WILD PUNCH

Turtle Point Press

NEW YORK

WILD PUNCH

Creston Lea

Copyright © 2010 by Creston Lea

Published by Turtle Point Press
www.turtlepointpress.com

ISBN 978-1-933527-40-6
LCCN 2009936139

Designed and composed by Quemadura

I am grateful to the editors of the following
publications, in which early versions of these
stories originally appeared: *DoubleTake*:
"Blackflies"; *Hunger Mountain*: "Debt";
Seven Days: "Silver Bells," "What Was Left";
25&Under/Fiction (Norton/DoubleTake
Books): "Indian Summer Sunday." —CL

for Kerrie and for Cora

WHAT WAS LEFT

BY ACCIDENT on day-off Friday after Thanksgiving, Lewis, whom everybody called Knot, found the old lost town in the worst and unlikeliest of spots, between mountains and near no good source of running water. He found the rows of cellar holes, filled up with tall bunches of white birch. He breathed hot air onto his hands and knew what he'd found. "I'm not stupid," he said right into the darkening sky. His teeth felt stale from coffee hours earlier.

The German Wirehair, a useless dog brought back by Knot's sister from her time in the Air Force, had run off on the Tuesday before, chasing a strong whitetail deer she would never catch. Knot found her tracks in the first sticking snow. Her prints were tight together: slow and cold. Then there she was, walking out from under some trees, eyes down like Knot was something she was practically bored with. "I see you," he said into her ear. He breathed into her nose and she licked him on the lips.

She watched Knot rub his palms together and carefully bring the plastic bag out of his jacket pocket. He laid the cold lumps of turkey stuffing out on the granite slab that had been someone's doorstep before the coming of scarlet fever or diphtheria or whatever had done it. She pushed at yesterday's food and then ate it down as fast as her stomach would allow.

Up above, Knot was saying, "Look what we found. Look what we found."

BLACKFLIES

JEFFREY AND I came upon the coyote at some hour past midnight, Jeffrey drunk and me driving. It was young, or small at least. Twenty pounds at most. It was there, right outside the kitchen door of my house, licking at the grass where I'd dumped the grease out of a bacon pan that morning and every morning. The headlights got him as we came over the rise and he skipped into the trees without looking up. Most animals will look up. Most animals will freeze under lights from a car. Jeffrey didn't even notice, but later he said it must have been hungry to stick around as long as it did. It's true, a coyote is shy.

JEFFREY HAD a brown bottle of beer out on the dashboard of his Skylark. He was sitting in the driver's seat, wearing his old high school basketball jersey to show off the new tattoo.

"Watch you don't end up in the ditch," his father said, grinning, coming out of the house with Laurel. He was wearing his softball uniform. There was still a big stripe of dirt down one leg from the last game. He had his cleats in his hands and boots on his feet and the elastic loops of his stirrups hung around his heels. They both had a look that said they'd gotten dressed in a rush. Laurel had her shoes in her hand too. She was only a couple of years older than me and a lot younger than Jeffrey's father. Jeffrey's mother had lit out from New Hampshire two years earlier. She'd been a secretary at the college. When the professor she loved took a new job in Lexington, Virginia, she went with him without any remorse, leaving Jeffrey's father behind to wonder what had happened. Jeffrey learned of his parents' separation by mail when he was in the Gulf.

The Skylark was green, a 1972 350 he bought from the town minister, battery dead from playing the radio where it sat in the yard. Jeffrey couldn't drive. His military driver's license didn't transfer to a regular driver's license. Which is why I had to drive him everywhere in my father's truck ever since he got discharged. He'd failed the written D M V test twice. I was the one who had to drive the car back from the minister's house in the first place. I was the one who put it right there under the butternut tree for all the butternuts to fall on. The grass was grown up under the undercarriage where Jeffrey couldn't mow when he did mow.

Laurel noticed the tattoo and broke off from Jeffrey's dad to take a look. He had taken off the wrap too early and there was a little dry blood around the edges.

"Well," she said, putting out a finger to touch, "that's colorful." The tattoo was a USMC eagle, globe, and anchor that said *Desert Demons* underneath in stencil letters.

"Laurel," his father said, "I'm not gonna be late." He looked at Jeffrey. "Watch that don't get infected," he said. "Put something to it or you'll be sorry." He nodded at me too, at the cut on my foot. Laurel got into her Toyota and started it up. A logging crew was working the woods below my parents' house that summer, above Jeffrey's place. They were clearing land for a string of new houses. Starting at sunrise, the trucks rumbled down the hill and flew past Jeffrey's house. It was illegal. There was a sign on the little bridge over the brook that said *Legal Load Limit 6 Tons*. They drove like there was nobody else on the narrow road. Laurel waited for the truck to speed past on its way back up to the log landing. The steel stakes on its empty trailer clanked around in their pockets as the tires rolled over the washboard ripples in the road. She waved her fingers at me as they backed down the driveway.

Dust was everywhere when they took off down the hill. It rose straight up and then drifted right into my face where I was sitting on the porch. I couldn't remember the last rain. It was the beginning of the summer, I was twenty-five, Jeffrey was a veteran, twenty-three years old. The air on a Saturday afternoon made you too lazy to do anything but sit there with your shoes off, rubbing the new bruise where a sick horse had stomped on your foot. It wasn't a bad year for blackflies—too dry or too hot, something. My own parents were gone off in the camper they bought at auction. The Grand Canyon, Old Faithful.

THIS WAS ALL back when I was first taking care of the gelding that the state had taken away from the Christian Scientists who had let him go gaunt and sick. You should have seen those people's barn stalls. Chewed to death. Same with all the trees on the place: bark stripped away from everything right down to the dirt. The grass was all eaten up and even the tree roots were bare from gnawing. Right after my parents left, the state split up the horses and I took in a three-year-old Arabian named Esau with bad teeth and shrunken hooves. I fed him and watered him down and generally saw after his welfare along with the other horses we kept. I was still living at home. I handled the cutting and selling of the hay from the fields myself, made a dollar seventy-five per bale and gave eighty cents on the dollar to my parents. My father had a good job and we were living well.

I'll admit it, I was mostly living off him. It was easy to do, then.

That same summer, King Bushey opened up a tattoo shop at his place on the River Road. By Appointment Only. Plenty of us that were young and watching the dry days pass went and got decorated by King's electric nee-dle. Even my father got his own name written inside a twisted scroll across his arm. I went with him and looked at King's drawings up on the wall while my father smoked Larks and King wiped away the blood, telling stories about when he was working down in Lebanon, clearing trees off the place where they put up the new hospital. He said everybody was stoned on marijuana and working like five hour days. They paid so much, he financed all the tattoo equipment with what he had left over at the end of the job, quit that heavy work forever.

He got his needle all ready to go again and rubbed Speed Stick deodorant on my arm and shaved it of its little hairs. I saw the blue and red crown tattoo on his forearm.

Because the ink is permanent, my arm still bears the likeness of three horses riding right out at you with all the speed you can imagine.

Jeffrey became vexed with jealousy when he saw it and had me drive him down to King's place immediately but King was booked solid and Jeffrey had to wait. Two weeks later, when Esau took a bad turn, I drove Jeffrey down to King's and went back to the barn to meet Ivy. Esau's thin under-eyelid had slipped partway down and I worried about moon-blindness or worse—things I had only read about. Before long, his whole eye was shut. For the days I'd had him, I'd kept him in a stall up in the new part of the barn for quarantine until he could get all his shots so the other horses wouldn't catch strangles or whatever else. Daytimes, I put him out in the paddock behind the barn after I'd gotten all the other horses into the lower fields, away from him. The Christian Scientists never gave them any shots. In court, they said it was freedom of religion, but everybody thought they were using that as an excuse for not bothering. It seemed like they had the money. When I first brought him up to our barn, he so glutted at his food, I had to put big rocks in the bucket with the feed to keep him from wolfing it all at once. But by the time his eyes swelled up and leaked dampness onto the short hairs of his face, he was hardly touching food. He hadn't opened up his eye in two days. I called Ivy on the barn phone.

The summer after twelfth grade, when she was home from college, Ivy and I spent a few nights together in the field behind her parents' place. But I generally don't know how to talk to girls. The phone went quiet and she said, "That horse is actually sick, right?"

She had agreed, out of charity, to provide attention to all the sick horses taken from the Christian Scientists. The animal people's national fund paid for shots. Ivy testified to the horses' poor medical condition in court. The lawyer called her by her real name, Lillian Hayes. I had almost forgotten that Ivy was a made-up name. My parents and I went to the North Haverhill courthouse and watched. All three of us put our names on a list of volunteers for taking on a sick horse. Ivy's smart. She talked to the judge like she'd done that a million times.

On the phone, she told me to block off the light and talk to Esau to keep him calm. Jeffrey appeared when I was up on the ladder hanging horse blankets over the windows. He stood there in the bright square of the sliding door, wearing his high school basketball jersey, ready to have King carve into his arm. The jersey was tight over what remained of his military muscle.

Jeffrey said, "He sick?" I could hear the disappointment in his voice.

"He's got something in his eye, but Ivy won't show up for another hour. There's nothing I can do yet except for make it dark. I'll still run you down to King's."

I nailed the blue blanket over the window and made it dark. Jeffrey went into Esau's stall. I heard the horse blow, stamp, turn.

"You'd better leave him alone," I said. "He's all nervous."

"I won't hurt him."

"Yeah, well, he can't see you at all."

"Me either," he said. "I can hardly see anything."

We went back into the light and drove my father's

Ford into town and then down into the river valley to where King's place sits on the flood plain. With the wind coming in the window, the heat went away. We didn't talk at all, just watched the faded gray pavement of the state road and the yellowing fields and the green, green woods. The river was low. From King's dooryard, you could see the water's stain high up on the opposite bank, below the sand cliff where kingfishers flew in and out of holes to dive into the water. I parked next to the leaning pole of the basketball hoop King built for his kids. Jeffrey started fidgeting in the seat. He was rubbing the spot on his arm where the tattoo would go.

He saw me noticing and stopped. "Semper Fi," I said. "Do or die."

He shook his head and smiled down at his feet.

IVY'S VET TRUCK was idling in front of the barn when I came back over the rise. The door to the barn was pulled shut except for an inch or two where a yellow extension cord ran in from a special plug on the side of her truck.

The sun was full-up by then, just hanging there. A spitbug was off making its whiny whistle someplace.

In the shade of the run-in stall below the barn, the

appaloosas we boarded, Speedy and Dumpling, were standing silently side by side, flicking their tails over each other's noses to whisk off the flies. They belonged to summer people. It was too hot for them to come up and ride their horses under the sun, to leave from wherever they lived, where there was air-conditioning and cold drinks. Both horses were growing round from still days spent below the barn. They were resigned to the heat in the dusty shadows, switching their tails in a constant rhythm. The other horses were out of sight, but I knew they'd be ganged together down in the shade at the bottom of the lower field.

"Ive?" I said into the dark. I could see the glow from her mechanic's hooklight from where it lay in the wood shavings on the stall floor. "I'm back."

"He looks bad. I need your help getting his eye open." I couldn't tell if I saw her shape in the dark or not. I imagined I could. "Get a halter and tie him."

I felt for the halter and line where they hung on a hook and felt my way into the stall. Esau huffed and stamped twice. I could hear Ivy whispering to him. She had the light turned toward the wall so it was just a glow there. It showed the whorls in the grain of the pine boards through their dark creosote stain.

Esau threw his head as I slid the halter past his eyes and over his ears. Ivy and I said, "Easy . . ." at the same time.

I said, "Remember when I stained these walls and the creosote in the oil made my skin puff up like air bubbles?"

"I remember you telling me about it." I felt her hand touch mine and she took the braided lunge line away from me. She snapped one end to a ring on the halter and then I heard the soft clicking sound of the line being pulled around one of the stall bars as she tied it off. "Hold his head," she said. "Talk to him."

Ivy adjusted the light so it lit up the wall all the way to the ceiling. There were spider webs I hadn't seen before. In the new light, I could see her opening a case and taking something out. She came up on the other side of his head. "You've got to talk to him. He can't see." She said, "That's a good boy," and "Easy does it" as she stroked his neck. I smoothed his shoulder and held the halter below his jaw. His ribs made a washboard, the skin between the bones dipping in far enough to fit two fingers. I saw her hands come up and touch the places around the horse's big closed eye. She was holding something. He stamped and I moved my feet back. When she brought her hands down to the eyelid, Esau tossed his head and I lost my hold on the halter. He struck out with his hoof and caught the stall door. It made a gunshot sound banging against the latch. One of the horses below the barn whinnied at the noise and Esau spun until his head was jerked back by the lunge line. His hind leg, with its small malnutritioned hoof, came down on my boot and I thought I felt my big toe split from my foot entirely. It made my ears fill up and I felt my mouth open all the way but not make any sound. All I could see was the yellow from Ivy's lamp.

I USED THIS BOTTLE when a cat scratched the living shit out of my arm," she said, showing me the pale, hair-thin ridges on her forearm before going back to painting brown stripes over my foot with antiseptic. "It's been in the glove box ever since."

I was sitting on the step, my blood-stained sock and boot wet under the dripping spigot.

"Maybe I shouldn't have, but I gave him steroid cream. That might help his eyes, but I'd keep the windows covered and the door shut anyways. You can use the lights to check on him." I could see the flecks of wood shavings stuck in her hair when she leaned over to roll a bandage around my foot. She had the straightest hair —it grew out of a line in the middle of her head and dropped right down the sides. She screwed the cap back onto the bottle. "You might have broken that toe, I don't know. I don't think they can do much for a broken toe, but you might want to get it looked at." She checked the watch she wore on the underside of her wrist. "If we go now, I can drop you at the clinic."

I wanted to ask her to stay for a while. She smelled like the molasses they put in grain. I said, "That's okay." She'd already called down to King's for me, said Jeffrey would have to find another ride home. Her truck was loaded with things I knew nothing about.

"Put it under some ice and take something to keep it from swelling up."

I thought about touching her hair, but she stood up before I could decide. "He might have tetanus, you know."

I nodded. I didn't know.

"I gave him penicillin last week, but if he got it before I gave him the shot, he's in trouble. Some of those horses were eating their own muck, so maybe, he could have it. If he has tetanus . . . I hope he doesn't. Watch him, okay?"

IT WAS AFTER she was gone, after I'd found the cane in the basement from when my father cut his leg with the chainsaw, after I'd pulled some porkchops out of the freezer to thaw for supper, after I'd had gone back up to the barn to look in on Esau that I saw the coyote's leavings by the barn door. Right there where I'd been sitting. Ivy hadn't noticed either. Shavings from when the farrier had last filed the horses' hooves lay everywhere; they looked like porcupine quills. A few of the thick U-shaped rinds of hoof that had been clipped away before the filing sat in the tall grass and two black pieces of coyote shit lay there, dusty and full of hair from some animal. I checked Esau and shut the door tight.

I HAD TO DRIVE with my bandaged foot up on the gear box, working the pedals with my left, slowly down to Jeffrey's. So slow that I could hear the bugs in the fields, whirring and peeping. A chipmunk raced me down the length of a stone wall. Sweat made my shirt stick to my back, made my back stick to the seat of the Ford.

I had to fight down a smile when I saw him there in the Buick with his tattoo and bottle of beer, trying to look like something from the television or a movie screen. He didn't quite look at me as I swung out of the truck.

"That's real nice," I said. "Sorry I couldn't pick you up."

"Yeah," he said, lowering his arm down from the window edge. "What happened to your foot?"

"Esau stomped me. Ivy took care of it." He raised his eyebrow at the mention of her name.

"Broke?"

I shook my head no and pulled myself up onto the porch. A butternut fell from the tree and made a watery sound on the roof of the Skylark. Jeffrey rolled his eyes and put his arm back up on the door. He blew on the tattoo like he was cooling it off. The thing about Jeffrey is that he spent his Marine Corps time sweating on the deck of a big iron ship twenty miles offshore in the Persian Gulf. He just hung around the kitchen and lifted weights and waited until they pulled anchor and shipped home. He didn't have very many stories. He still lied about girls.

"That coyote's back. I found its shit by the barn, like maybe he was after the hoof clippings off the horses. Dogs will eat those things up, so, he might too."

Jeffrey nodded. "There's something in them they like."

Laurel's Toyota was parked right behind the Skylark, where the grass was only medium-length. Her license plate said Z O S O.

That was when I heard Jeffrey's father and Laurel inside the house. She was laughing and he walked by the screen door behind me two or three times before they came out together, him wearing his soiled softball uniform and carrying his cleats. Jeffrey saw Laurel and shifted in the seat so the tattoo would be more obvious. Jeffrey's father saw this and nodded to the long grass grown up around the tires, under the car. He ran his tongue under his upper lip.

That was when he said, "Watch you don't end up in the ditch."—When he looked down and nodded to me, saw the moon-shaped bruise on my foot, the pile of gauze wrap with brown ink-spots of blood. Laurel slipped out from his arm to go see Jeffrey's tattoo. She was carrying her shoes and I saw how she walked on tip-toes across the gravel. It made the muscles in her calves bunch up.

A log truck blew by on the road, dust rising up behind it. They backed out onto the road and were gone.

We sat there like that, me on the porch, him in his stationary used car, all afternoon, going nowhere. There were hardly any blackflies at all. In the early evening, tired from the heat and stillness, I let Jeffrey drive my dad's truck back up the hill to the house. He did fine, just got a little bit nervous when a loaded truck came around a bend up ahead of us. He turned a little too fast into the sandy turnaround at the side of the road and I bumped my sore foot against the door. We rolled our windows up quick against the dust. When everything settled down enough to see, Jeffrey made up for his skittishness by stylishly rolling the steering wheel back around with his palm before letting it slide back through his fingers on its own. It was something I was supposed to notice.

Jeffrey cooked the porkchops with Coca-Cola and half a bottle of lime juice. He made a mess with the pots and pans, all the spices. The sun went down on the other side of the hills and left behind the soft light that we have late into summer evenings. When it was time to put the meat in the oven for a while, Jeffrey and I went to the barn. My foot had started to hurt in a new way and I had to lean on the cane, which was a few inches too short, and which made me hobble worse than I would have otherwise. I could feel the hurt on the bottom of my foot as well as the top. Down the hill, the log crew shut down for the night and I realized how I didn't even notice the sound any more. Somewhere in the woods, somebody honked his horn, saying goodnight.

The barn was dusty and hot from the windows being shut all day long. It made Jeffrey sneeze four times in a row. He found his way to the feed room and dropped a new bale of woodshavings through the trapdoor to the run-in stalls below the barn. I heard him yell down at the appaloosas, "Move it!" before he pushed the bale down to where they stood. He'd done it a hundred times, I didn't have to tell him how. Light leaked out from the feed room door and I saw Esau straining his nose up and away from his body, turning at the neck in the slowest, stiffest way.

I got the stall door open and put my hand out for his nose. He breathed hard and strained from deep down in his throat, twice together, too fast, and then didn't breathe. He twitched his nose away from my hand, but just barely, like he was frozen there, legs stiff and out in all four directions for support.

Jeffrey was singing some little song to himself. He shut off the light and I heard the door creak. I heard his footsteps and then another light came on. I put my hand on Esau's nose. The skin is so soft there. A puff of hot air breezed across my palm from his nostril and I ran my hand over his neck, down to the shoulder, over the muscles that were tensed like he was pushing against something. He was sweating like he'd been running hard. Jeffrey shut off the light. He was carrying a shovel and his boots made a one-two-three rhythm with the shovel blade as he came across the wood floor of the barn.

I said, "Call Ivy," and he didn't hear me right the first time. When he said, "What?" and I said it again, I must have said it loud because later I remembered hearing him stop moving, like he was going to ask what was wrong. Then I heard him fumbling with the doorlatch to the tack room. The light switched on and I heard him dialing the old wall-mount phone, trying to force the slow dial back faster than it wanted to go. It made a little straining noise. Esau let out two more short breaths and stretched his jaw out again, bobbing his muzzle. His eye was open now, and even in the half-light, I could see the milky undereyelid covering most of his big glass eye. I put my arms around the thick of his neck, felt the hot wetness of his hair, the ridges of his full-up veins. His tail was raised.

It took Ivy twenty minutes to get to us. It can take almost thirty even if you take your chances and haul ass down Route 10 from up around her place to mine. Jeffrey and I were busy sponging Esau's neck with the big porous sea sponges my mother had bought somewhere. We had taken the blankets off the windows to soak and cover him, Jeffrey running them out to the water trough and dragging them back in, heavy with sun-warmed water. Esau had laid down hard, body first, then his neck and head. Even on his side, his legs stuck out stiff like they were made out of wood.

Jeffrey had said "poor boy" about twenty million times since then, squeezing the sponge over Esau's face and neck the way Ivy had told him to do on the phone. I couldn't help but flinch every time Esau took a breath. My jeans were soaked through from sitting on the floor in the mix of wood shavings and water. By the time Ivy's tires sounded on the gravel of the driveway, it was dark enough for her headlights to light up the trees on the other side of the window. Esau may have already quit breathing. I can't be sure.

IVY ASKED US if we'd wait outside while she gave him the shot. I felt like I was supposed to protest but I didn't want to. It's not something I really wanted to see.

So Jeffrey and I went out to sit on the grass. It wasn't a bad year for blackflies. A few landed on my arms, tried to nestle into my tear ducts. I pushed my finger tips against them and they were gone.

Jeffrey was lying on his back with his hands over his eyes. He said, "It's coming up on a year since I got back. I haven't done shit."

I rubbed at my foot and didn't say anything. The barn's silhouette looked like a big black hole in the evening sky.

He said, "You know I've been with Laurel a few times," and this time I knew he was telling the truth.

"We're talking about leaving together."

I said, "Where would you go?" but it came out more like a breath. I don't know if he heard me.

"We might go down to where my mom's at. She says it's nice down there. There's work too. I could get off my ass."

I said, "Uh huh," but I was really just staring into the black hole in the sky, the first few stars around its edges. Ivy stepped out of the blackness and sat down between us. She rubbed at her neck with her fingers.

She said, "Animals die." And then she said it again.

After a while she stood up to go. She looked at me for a minute and I stood up too. "I'll come by tomorrow," she said. "I'll bring a halter to bury him with if you like. Unless he's got one that's his own. I've got one. I'd like to." I nodded that that would be good, but I didn't really understand. She was chewing on her lower lip a little bit.

Jeffrey called, "Bye Ivy," and she turned in the dark to say bye back to him, but it sounded funny because I was standing right next to her and she was aware of me. She put her hands in her pockets and took them out again. "I'll see you tomorrow," she said.

JEFFREY TOOK the burnt porkchops out to the edge of the yard, to where the trees begin but where we could still see under light from the moon. We sat on the porch all night waiting to see if the coyote would be brave enough to come take them away.

We never saw it, but when the sun came up, I took the cane and walked across the yard. The meat was gone, of course. Jeffrey was there on the porch, asleep on the lawn chair where he'd been sitting all night. It was just beginning to get hot again. Another summer day. His basketball shirt was dirty from the night before and it made him look young and old. How could he have known Laurel would break his heart two times? That she would put his father in the hospital down in Lebanon by running her car against a tree, ducking a flying log truck on a tight corner? That she would leave them both, then? Jeffrey, who would abandon his father in the expensive hospital to reenlist in the Marines. Jeffrey, who is in Haiti now, part of something neither Ivy nor I understand.

I let him sleep and walked up to the barn. Its metal roof reflected the morning sun into my eyes and it hurt to look.

LET THE SAD

TIMES ROLL ON

ODESSA WAS BORN and raised by grandiose, oil-wealthy parents all over the world: Saudi Arabia. Alberta, Canada. Houston and West Texas. Her teachers in international schools and the nannies who spoiled her from the minute she was born, they gave her a complex accent that had nothing to do with anyplace. The number of times I asked, "What?" every day was astounding. You'd think that in time I'd have adapted to it, but she might as well have been talking in secret code. And, she talked fast. Adding to her particular allure, as far as I was concerned, were the many millions of brown freckles patterned all over her in a way that I'd never seen before. You might have even thought she was part-something, part-something else until you got up close and saw the freckles on her skin. She didn't look anything like other girls around here. I can comprehend that other people might not have seen her like I did, but I can't pretend I didn't light up the very minute she strode into the classroom.

At first, I was too aflame to care that we couldn't find a

way to get along. Many of us long for something *exotic* and I couldn't believe my good luck victory.

Insignificant things put us at odds.

For example, I had it mind to make for us an elaborate repast. Chicken cooked in wine. Artichokes. Like an all-four-burners event. I've worked plenty in restaurants and am capable in the kitchen. Things had been pretty good between us recently. At least not vicious like sometimes in the past. I thought we might get really close over some wine, sweet-talk, maybe leave the dishes on the table and lead each other by the hand into the bedroom.

I went to the store and bought what I needed, went across the river and picked up a good-looking bottle of Chianti because she likes it, not because it works with the chicken. I went home to the apartment, put on my Skeeter Davis tape and turned on the stove. She came home and gave me a look I'd seen before. There I am, in an apron.

"What's that face for?"

"You're wearing an apron?"

"Well, you might guess I'm cooking us some food."

"There's no need to be excited, I'm sure."

She put her coat on the rack and walked down to the

bedroom to change clothes while I stood there with an oven mitt on one hand and a rubber spatula in the other, looking at her back. "None for me, I ate in town."

"What do you mean you ate in town? I have fennel. I bought us wine."

She walked back past the television and the couch, pulling a clean black sweater down over her hips. "I already ate."

"Well why didn't you tell me before?"

"Before what?" Then she said something I couldn't understand and I gave her a blank face she'd seen before. It made her mouth tighten up and her head shake a little. "You heard what I said."

"If you're going to be unreasonable, you might as well do it in one of the recognized languages of the globe."

She went ahead and punched me right in the chest, right above the heart. I stood back and tried not to rub at the pain but in truth it made breathing a little difficult and I had to take hold of the refrigerator handle. I called her a name that was never meant to be spoken and she slapped her hand down on the counter hard enough to make the cookbook slowly fan its pages and then close itself. She is very tough and likely to throw whatever's close at hand, though usually more for show than with the intent to maim. After a few minutes' zesty vocal exchange, she slowly heaved the bottle of wine overhand almost like she was throwing it to me. I tried to catch it, but it flew off my fingertips and dented the sheetrock before falling heavily to the floor where it bounced on its neck. We stopped shouting for a moment to silently appreciate that it hadn't broken.

Blue lights flashed once around the apartment and we could see the gold-on-green cruiser slowing down to park across the street. She stepped past me to flick off the light switches by the door. I shut off the tape player and we both got down below the counter in the kitchen. We'd done it all before. It wasn't the way she was brought up to live.

There wasn't much room and we had to squeeze together down there in the dark. She smelled so fine, like always. We heard the sound of unhurried shoes coming up the steps and the static of a police radio crackling outside the door. I don't know why they always need to have them turned up so loud. Three loud, sharp, police-style knocks and then nothing but static and the muffled sound of a voice talking into a radio. Three more knocks and then footsteps down the steps and back across the street to the car. State cops. They get called in while they're speeding through town on 10 and seem to care very little about very much.

We hid there and faced facts.

We knew the end was near. It's terrible, that knowledge. It is the same knowledge I had at the end with Laurel and with Beth and will surely have with others down the road. It's always just a matter of time. Like the fuse is burning from the day you meet. Really, it's a mystery why she stayed as long as she did. Most of what I'd been doing was living off her while she went to school and taught a class at the college extension, the one where I'd found myself as a student for about five minutes before I decided that my little venture back to the realm of The Academics was not in the cards. But there, under the noisy fluorescent lights of the classroom, we began our fateful tale.

We laid there on the vinyl tiles and held onto each other and felt sad in a way that was more intimate than you might think when you consider that the whole reason we were sad in the first place was that we couldn't seem to function in the normal, loving way.

After a while, she got up and went back into the bedroom without saying a word and I was left in the kitchen, lying on the floor by myself. I reached down the corkscrew from the counter and got into the fallen bottle of wine for a few sips. The faucet was dripping into something in the sink, making a big sound in the quiet. I got up and put the chicken and butter and squeeze-ball of lemon juice away for some other day.

It was a nice night out. Cold, but warmer than it'd been in a while now that the sun was staying out later. There wasn't much action out on the street, just some cars going by on the other side of the trees and a cat digging around by the Dumpster. I sat down on the step and drank a couple more swallows of wine. There was a silhouette of a rooster on the label around the neck of the bottle. Some Italian farmer had grown grapes and squashed them down and five years later that bottle had ended up in my hands in New Hampshire. I heard on the radio about public baths in Turkey where you can get soap that's a hundred years old. They keep making it and what they make today won't get used for another hundred years. Somebody will use it to wash his neck and be done with it forever. I could have gone inside and talked it out but what's the use? We might have made each other feel better in the end, said some tearful words of affection and then indulged in some of the tired and particularly excellent loving that comes after battling and peacemaking. But I wasn't so sure that I felt like saying the words, "I don't know" over and over and over again for a couple of hours while we worked it out. We both knew it wouldn't last.

I put the bottle in the long grass next to the steps and went down to the sidewalk to look back at the apartment. It's the one apartment building in the whole town. It was new then. And ugly. And a byproduct of the college to the south. Things are creeping north into this town where I have lived forever. Most of the lights in the building were on and I wondered which of my caring neighbors called the cops without even so much as first knocking on our door. People just love to call the police. Our bedroom window went dark and I stared at the rectangle of darkness for a while before she turned on the lamp by the bed and the ceiling lit up a little bit. I knew she'd be writing in her diary. She always went to it after we'd had it out. I never saw her run to it after we'd had a good day —drop everything just to record my graciousness or sensitivity. Some nights she stayed up for an hour writing in her book, page after page after page.

The temptation to read her diary was something beyond my powers of restraint. All the unspoken facts. The truth laid bare! She didn't used to hide it back in the beginning. It just stayed wedged between dictionaries on her shelf. I'd sneak a peek every now and again, just to check my standing. It was pretty frustrating. I was out of work for a while there, which sometimes happens to me. The days had been long with nothing to do but change channels and flip through Odessa's *Marie Claire* magazines looking at the women inside. Eventually I came around to checking the diary every day—idle hands being what they are, and so on. All I got for a long time was one in green ink about a friend of hers back in Houston not being happy with her job in a bank. Then time went by and she wrote for pages, but it had almost nothing to do with me at all. It was all about her parents and her "sphere of understanding" and the people she works with at the college, where she was earning a master's degree in global economics. When finally I found my own name, it said that we'd gone down to the Royal Oak, a place that she hates, and that, "typically," I'd thought she was eyeballing Scott Snelling, who is a handsome fellow I grew up with and never much cared for. She *was* looking at him, too, I think, but she didn't even bother to write yes or no about it, which, of course, would have set the story straight. Maybe if she knew how fat he used to be, things would've been different. We didn't call him Boss Hogg for no reason. At times like those, sitting on the bed with her secret book in my hands, I wondered if true love would ever come my way, as the song goes.

Eventually, of course, I made a few slips. I didn't remember that some bit of information I knew about her had come from my mid-afternoon espionage. She began hiding it and, so help me, I couldn't find it anywhere. It's not like I was dealing with a vast amount of space. And I searched thoroughly, even with a flashlight. But then she'd have it again, sitting up in bed with her glasses on, writing steadily, never having to stop and think of what to put down next, me just lying there next to her. At times, I think she just decided to write and write until I passed over into sleep.

I was out there on the sidewalk, contemplating, when King Bushey honked his horn and cut across the street to where I stood so that his truck pointed down the road in the wrong direction. That's illegal on this side of the river.

"Get in. Let's go down to the Royal Oak for a while. I just got *paid*." King pulled a big roll of bills out of his shirt pocket, but they looked mostly like ones.

"Well. I don't know if that would go over so good."

"Bring her along. I got room." He ran his hand over the seat like the girls on *The Price Is Right* when they're making a toaster look sexy.

I turned around to look up at the bedroom window again and saw that the light had gone out. I'd never been one to just leave unannounced before.

"I guess I could go for a little while."

King drove slowly along the side roads. Everything was pretty quiet, not much action anywhere. He played a tape he'd made off his records at home. He's got a lot of records. I'd always sort of known who he was even though he grew up across the river. Musical affinity is how we got going as friends. I met him for real on a job down in Lebanon, unloading a truck full of forty-pound boxes into a storage building at the huge new hospital. As is usual, the radio on the dock played standard inflated FM nonsense and it was the source of a lot of agony for me. And, as usual, I lost some otherwise potential friends by mouthing off about their musical discriminations. But it introduced me to King, who likes all the same old songs I'd learned from my dad: Webb Pierce, Hank Snow, Bob Wills. I went up to his place after work one night and we played his Tammy Wynette tape and drank all his beer. That'll make you feel friendly with someone. He told me about how, coincidentally, he'd worked clearing the land where the hospital sits now. Making money hand over fist, he said. Nothing like the truck-unloading affair we'd both chanced into.

I think he made that name, King, up because he liked its rock 'n' roll connotations. I have seen his old union card from when he was a groundskeeper at the college, the one that says Glenn Bushey. He is Canadian by birth, I think, but doesn't say so. Eventually, he got a pile of money when his grandmother died and switched to tattooing full-time.

"Maybe me and O.D. have had it."

His smirk said, *Again?* I chose to ignore it.

"Somebody called the cops on us tonight. It's embarrassing. I'm embarrassed."

"First off, you ought to learn to control your volume."

"They ought to learn to control their ears. Everybody is in a such big hurry to call the cops. It's not like we were being *that* loud. People move into an apartment building and expect it to be quiet as a churchmouse. I can hear the girl upstairs doing exercises and I don't call in the cops on her do I?"

I knew it amused him that she threw objects at me from time to time so I kept quiet about it.

"There's nothing in it for her, I know, but I *try* and do nice things. I was going to make supper. I swear to God, if we can fight over that we can fight over anything."

After a while, King said, "It does sound to me like she might have a different explanation." I knew it was as true as anything I could have said back to him.

At a stop light, we came up behind a little Nissan with Massachusetts plates and a mysterious sticker across the trunk that said NO GRAPES!!

The Royal Oak was empty of people I recognized. Sometimes I get an idea that everybody but me has heard about something better. Or maybe something worse: an imminent natural disaster or plague causing them to flee from town, leaving me to perish all alone with nobody left for company except for maybe King or whoever else is hanging around the Royal Oak. Which meant, that night, a bartender named Brian and a bunch of younger kids I had never seen before sitting over by the clackity-clackity pinball machine which every now and then lit up and said, "Ride the Ferris wheel!" King left me almost immediately to stand beside the pool table in the back room with somebody I didn't know. I ordered a beer and punched in a few songs on the jukebox while Brian got my drink from beneath the sliding door of the cooler. Of course the selection wasn't ever much to behold at the Royal Oak, but they had a Sun Records greatest-hits and a Buck Owens CD called *I've Got a Tiger by the Tail,* which King bought specifically to give to the Royal Oak. I put two quarters in and called up Charlie Rich, "Midnight Blues" and Jerry Lee Lewis's "Crazy Arms" before sitting back down to drink my drink.

The Royal Oak used to be different. By law, you had to buy your alcohol through a window outside and bring it in through the door to drink it. Maybe find yourself standing in the sleet, the snow, the dark of night waiting for a Singapore Sling. But now it's just like anywhere else.

Sooner or later, King came back holding a pool cue

and took a stool next to mine. I mostly quit smoking about a year before, but I still occasionally yielded to that particular vice. I got one off King and he held up his lighter for me.

"Surviving?" he asked.

"I don't know. It's like, if it's going to be over, let's just make it over. I don't want to go through all the usual business. I've done that one too many times already. We just weren't cut out for each other's company is all there is. She's not even from here."

I could tell King had forgotten about my problems with Odessa and wasn't expecting a serious answer to his query. He looked back at the pool table and bounced the end of his cue off the floor between his feet a few times before turning back to the bar.

"You better think on it before you do something big and find yourself alone every day and wishing you had her around." He made a jerking-off motion with his fist.

I looked over at the younger kids to check whether they saw him doing that. If they did, I couldn't tell.

"This cigarette is killing me." I ground it out in the blue Labatt ashtray and slid it away down the bar. "Why do you let me do this to myself? I thought you were supposed to be my friend."

"Oh, I *am* friendly, which is why I gave it to you in the first place and also is why I'm telling you to think for a few minutes. What're you gonna do? Move out? Get a job? It might be hard to find another like her." Somebody back in the pool room called to him that he was due at the table and he started walking. He spun around on his heel and said, "'Specially for you" and walked past the juke-box to where pool players stood around leaning on cues, waiting for him and wondering who I might be.

"Oh is that right?" I said to his back.

I ordered another beer and paid for it out of the short stack of bills I had slowly soaking up wetness on the bar. I'd been odd-jobbing here and there, pruning trees and a little painting, but it was too early to cut grass and too late to plow snow and I was running slightly low. It was something I needed to try to do something about.

Next thing I knew, I was feeling sort of clumsy and it'd gotten late. I was also out of money. I recalled that I never did eat anything for supper, which explained the bad feeling in my stomach. Brian was busy restocking bottles and I got him to float me a bag of corn chips. I knew Odessa would definitely be asleep by then. In fact, she was probably closer to waking up than bedding down, but I couldn't make out the clock from where I sat and

Brian is as often as not inclined to ignore the State's wishes on the subject of closing time if he's making money. I wasn't really all that excited about going home and trying to be silent while getting into bed. Nor was I thrilled by the notion of waking up all hung over and having to face her in that state while she got ready to go to teach a classroom full of the young and vibrant while I prepared to idle away another day.

I knew I'd search for her diary some more in the morning, just to gauge the depth of her anger and the truth of her feelings. Better to know what she thought before saying something I couldn't take back. If a decision needed making, I didn't want to make it alone.

I went back to the pool room to check up on King, but there was nobody there except some fellows playing pool with some girls. They looked collegiate. He was nowhere to be found.

In the bathroom, there were two men pissing next to each other. One at the urinal and one at the toilet. The man at the urinal turned away from the wall first, which pleased me. But just when I was about to advance, the man at the toilet took a step sideways to the urinal, pissing a line across the wall in transit. He was a great big horse of a dude in a checked blazer coat, sideburns down to his mouth, head leaned back as he gazed up to the pipes on the ceiling. I worried that I'd freeze up like I sometimes do in these situations, out in the open with someone else listening for the sound of water hitting water. But I was drunk enough to not care a whole lot and things went as they are meant to. He was still standing there at the urinal when he said, "You're obviously a man who pees well. You should be up at The Hilltop having a real beer."

I didn't know what to say to something like that, so I just zipped up and walked out, deciding it was time to find King and go home before I fell down.

He was gone. I sat back down at the bar and tried to figure out what to do next. Just like King to ditch me way out at the Royal Oak with no money. Just like me to be there. I dreaded the idea of calling Odessa and waking her up to ask for a ride because I could already see her face when she'd pull up outside and I'd have to get in and be thankful. I knew she'd just be quiet and make me suffer until I'd say, "Will you talk to me?" Then she'd get to answer, "You can't understand me anyway."

I was busy checking through my pockets for a quarter

to call home when one of the girls from over by the pinball machine came up and asked me for a cigarette.

"Oh, I'm sorry," I said. "I don't smoke."

"I saw you smoking earlier."

"No, that was my friend's cigarette. I quit almost a year ago. Eleven months April first."

"Well, you aren't doing a real good job of it, 'cause I saw you smoke a cigarette a while back."

I tried to determine if she was pretty or not and decided she might have looked a little better somewhere else. But she had on a blue and yellow sideways-striped shirt that I liked the looks of. And white jeans. That's something I hadn't seen in quite a while. I thought she might not be from the college after all. "What've you, been watching me?" I said, trying to sound a little sly. But I was pretty worn out to be sly. I could hear it in my own voice.

"No, my friend was watching your sidekick. They took off while you were asleep on the bar."

"I wasn't asleep on any bar."

"Okay. I'm blind then. You ought to go home and go to bed."

"No. Well, you know. Well, my friend drove me. He left? Positive?"

"That's what I just said. He tried to roust you up but you just waved him off."

"Oh."

She had her back turned halfway toward me, looking down the bar for someone drawing on a cigarette. There were more people in there than I'd realized.

"They coming back?"

"I wouldn't count on it." She dug a couple of bills from her front pocket and put a foot on the rail, resigned to buying an expensive pack of cigarettes from behind the bar. Brian saw her and held up a finger meaning *just a second* while he finished squirting soda into a tall glass from the snake that runs down to tanks below the bar.

"Hey, you didn't happen to come here in a car, did you? If you wanted, we could carpool."

She didn't like the sound of that, I could tell right off. "Maybe your friend is coming back for you. He probably is. So, you don't have any cigarettes on you, do you?"

"I live right on 10." But she was already halfway back to the pinball machine. I can't blame her. A woman's got to be careful about talking to just anybody.

I was fairly resigned to calling Odessa and accepting my fate in her anger. In a way I figured that a moonlight drive might help to speed up the inevitable. It occurred to me that perhaps I would be doing us a great service. But then, upon further consideration, it also occurred to me that perhaps not.

I resolved to spend on the jukebox the last quarter I was going to leave for Brian as a tip, give King another five minutes to feel remorseful and come back for me.

I got a number punched in. It was Ray Charles singing, "It brings a tear into my eyes . . ." and the sound of the horns pulled the last of my strength right out through my knees. They were cumbersome questions I was asking of myself while I leaned my hands on the brightly lit glass of the jukebox and listened.

Maybe I shut my eyes again, I don't know. But the next thing that happened was I felt a fatherly hand pressing on my shoulder and looked up to see the sideburned fellow from the bathroom. His hair was all wet and hanging down in his face. I saw that it must have been raining out. What he said to me was this: "Have you ever wrestled a giant baby?"

"Pardon me?"

"I'll be out back, gray Chevelle."

And then he was gone. It was more than I could even comprehend, leaning there against the jukebox listening to men I'll never see with my own eyes play sad notes on an old record made before I was born. It's a typical and pathetic posture, I knew even then.

The next hand I felt on my shoulder belonged to Odessa. She held onto me and asked me if I was okay.

"I'm okay."

"King called me. You want to go back home?"

"Okay." I said, "Let's go home."

She drove me back through the rain to our apartment. Then she helped me up the stairs, out of my clothes, and into bed. Those are the things she did for me without my asking. For those, I said, "Thank you," and meant it. Then she said something I didn't understand, but it told me that what we had between us wasn't over yet.

I AM SO FUCKING

RETARDED

ODESSA LEFT TOWN so fast after finishing school, she didn't even wait for her diploma. It arrived a week later in a cardboard mailer from the college. I opened it and set it on my table as a keepsake. There were words printed in Latin on the heavy paper behind plastic. A thin sheet of paper almost like tissue was sandwiched in the booklet and I had to be careful moving it aside so it wouldn't rip. I hoped she'd call and ask for it.

It was June and summer had come fast without turning back into winter for a while the way it usually does. It was warm without being too hot. Bright blue days. A few of her friends called from here and there, asked for her. I would tell them she was gone, and they would say *Oh* . . . and then hang up, not so sure what they ought to say to me. I suppose they knew our end was coming. We all did. It's something I've commented on before.

She went to San Francisco, California: the City By The Bay. She said there was a job waiting for her, which proves she knew she was leaving for a while before she actually went. I didn't argue. I was surprised it lasted as long as it did. In a couple of days, she was gone out the door. Her sudden departure off to the other side of America was just an affirmation that I was only a stop-over for her.

I had bought another car by that point, an AMC Eagle station wagon. It had been the cruiser for the town police officer when it was new fifteen years ago. It'd had a couple of owners since then. One of them had peeled the shields off the sides, but you could make out the dark spots where they had been. There was steel mesh separating the back seat from the front, and you couldn't open the back doors from the inside. I'd ridden back there once when I was sixteen or seventeen, some time before I came to understand that actions had consequences. I took the mesh out, but I saved it behind the couch in case I changed my mind. Sometimes I would drive around with my arm hanging out the window, go over by the river where there were still wide lakes of water standing in some of the cornfields. Other times I would drive to the Royal Oak, which was empty of college students, more or less, for the summer.

The Cyclone pinball game was gone from the Royal

Oak, too. It had been there for years and years. I never dreamed it could go. Instead, there was a newer one with a picture of Sylvester Stallone and some other people. It made computer sounds and was too easy. I got sick of it after the first week.

This was around the time that I hated to go home to the apartment. Odessa had come to town from North-ampton, Massachusetts and hadn't brought much with her, but after she left it seemed like the place was empty. She left two boxes of books sitting on the TV table, and I hadn't figured out what to do with them so there they sat. The closet was where she'd kept her clothes, so it was empty except for my suit coat and good shoes. The closet was an afterthought in the apartment: walls nailed right into the carpet and butted up against the acoustic ceiling tiles. There wasn't even a real door, but Odessa had hung up a square of pretty fabric which she took with her when she left. It looked like a doorway to a wall now.

The Eagle had a decent-sized back seat, and you could fold it down to make even more room. I fit in it pretty well. On nights I went to the Royal Oak alone, I could park in back, on a flat spot behind a forsaken Tip-

Top Bread truck, and wake up there in the morning. It became something to look forward to. I had a sleeping bag and a small alarm clock that prevented me from sleeping past a reasonable hour and ensured that I'd get to work on Whipple Hill Road, dismantling my uncle's yellow house which had sat among the Christmas tree rows forever. It had been empty for quite some time. The cracked asphalt shingles had allowed grimy water to run down the walls of most rooms upstairs, making the wallpaper peel off in layers and the plaster sag underneath. The oldest part of the house had wide white pine floorboards that I tore up carefully-carefully and sold to a wood broker from Brattleboro named Yves. He'd leave a trailer parked in the yard and I'd stack floorboards there until it was loaded down onto the relief springs. I used lumber tarps he'd left behind to guard the wood from rain. Yves would come get the trailer and leave an empty one for me to load. He'd park it closer to the part of the house where I was working then. Depending on width versus length, he paid more or less five dollars a board foot, which he estimated by tape measure without the help of a scaling stick like I've seen at mills and lumber yards before. Then he'd roll off again to resell the wood for a million billion dollars. He'd sold barns to two members of Aerosmith and an actress from the movie *Addams Family Values* before.

I got twenty-five hundred dollars in green money for each of the first two trailer loads by working just six hours a day with a break for lunch. I took the cash to the bank inside the hardware store and got a cashier's check for twelve-hundred-fifty-dollars each time, sent that to my uncle in Florida. The rest went into a drawer in the kitchen. I could withdraw my hand from within while clutching several different fifty dollar bills at once. I bought the Eagle and was free to drive down the road.

It seemed like there was nobody to see. I worked in the morning until noon, ate a sandwich in the car, played the radio and smoked the second half of the joint I'd begun in the morning. Then what? Drive around, read a book Willie Nelson wrote about himself, watch television, swim in the cold water at the pond among the little kids there for swimming lessons while the same company of wrinkly women sat in beach chairs working on their tans day after day. They'd been there since I could remember, smoking long women's cigarettes which were handy for burning off leeches when the need arose. I wrote a letter to Odessa and tore it up and wrote another one and put it in the drawer with the money. With the days getting longer and plenty of time on my hands, it became clear how many people had left me behind.

At night, there was television and there was the Royal Oak.

Eventually Yves's trailer was parked in the long grass at the back of the house and I lowered the boards down gently from the window above, walking across the exposed joists to get there, making sure not to step off onto the lath and plaster that formed the ceiling below. I was a long way from anybody who could help if I got hurt. I found a little brass token of some sort, a key, and a handful of old coins tucked here and there amongst the plaster dust. Down on the ground, I carefully tapped the old rosehead nails out of the floorboards and put them in a coffee can. I stacked the last boards top-face to top-face with lath between layers to keep air between them and ratcheted the load straps down tight enough to hold it all together. It was five in the afternoon on a Friday when I finished. I made tracks.

The sun was still high, and the light on the trees in the woods made them look like you could walk in and lie down among the pine needles and shadows, be content for ever after. It was early enough in the summer that the undergrowth hadn't snarled itself into a mass like you had to fight to penetrate. The dirt roads were packed down shiny and as hard as blacktop.

By the time I made it home to call Yves and make a withdrawal from the cash drawer, the sky had begun going a little gray. By the time I rolled into the Royal Oak's lot, dark clouds had started to bunch up. Inside, there were a few people sitting at a table. Others were playing pool, hanging around the jukebox. A Red Sox game was being played on the silent television up on the wall. Three girls were at the bar with their heads together. Shifting light from the big front window cast a beam that cut through the dark room—dust hovered like millions of tiny bugs in the swath, moving around but immune to gravity. I was regarding it when I heard laughing at the bar.

Brian was leaning on his elbow, talking to the girls by the taps. He was tugging at the front of his T-shirt collar, which meant he was making sure his back hair wasn't showing. He looked up at me settling down on a stool and I knew he was hoping I would move off to a table for a while so he could continue to talk to the girls without me in the near distance. They looked to be having a pretty good time. He turned and fished a Budweiser out of the cooler behind him and walked the length of the bar before twisting off the cap and setting it down in front of me. I'd tried his patience many times in the past.

Brian twitched the top two bills off the stack of three I'd left on the bar and gestured over his shoulder toward the clock, "Happy hour." He threw the beer cap sidearm into a cardboard box with a plastic liner.

It wasn't any Happy Hour any more. I took it as a sign that Brian wasn't pissed at me, but didn't want any hassle either. I left the dollar out so he could see I meant it as a goodwill tip.

The girls were about my age. One looked like Michelle Strout, a girl I went to school with until the eighth grade. She went to a different high school, so I couldn't be sure. They had a piece of paper out and were laughing at what they drew there. Brian pushed a towel over the dry bar and laughed too.

I made shapes on the bar with the wet base of the bottle: the Olympic, the Audi, the Ballantine Ale. There were words carved into the bartop that had been there a long time, painted over. With the dying sun coming into the darkness and just the click of pool balls, the computer sounds from the pinball machine, some giggling, it was hard to imagine the Royal Oak crowded with drinkers, the jukebox playing, somebody carving his name into the bar: Buglet, Beaver, Quazar. It was quiet enough that I felt funny even looking up from my bottle. But then there was a big round of laughter and the girls were holding each other's shoulders. Brian was standing up straight biting his lip in a way that showed he was trying to not look like a fool, turning the bar towel over in his hands.

The girls were really busting a gut, eyes closed laughing out loud, gasping for breath. I started to think maybe two of them were sisters, if one resembled the father and the other one the mother. Brian looked down the bar at me and rubbed the towel over nothing, started to say something to them and then stopped. Then he said, "Ask him," and snapped his towel in my direction.

The girl I thought I knew snatched up the paper and spun backwards off the stool to come at me kind of hunched over and grinning. I wondered then if they hadn't been there for quite a while already, experiencing happy hour in its entirety. She was wearing a red shirt with a wide open neck that showed her collarbones. Her hair curled in on the sides in a way that meant she worked on it in front of a mirror. She sat down on the stool around the bar corner from me and fell onto both elbows. I said, "Are you Michelle Strout?"

"Yes of course," she said in one breath. "What does this say."

I looked at the paper in her hand. It was a little wet from the bartop and there were places where the ink had run out a bit in the moisture. There were nonsense words that said:

EYE HAM SOFA KING

WE TODD ED

Odessa used to make fun of the way I move my lips when I read to myself. I tried to resist doing that.

"No, read it out loud." Her two friends were leaning up on the bar like they were trying to forget about the stools altogether. Brian moved a little closer to them and I knew he was counting the long hours until he could close up, trying to gauge whether he could keep at least one of their bunch there until then. I looked at Michelle

Strout waiting for me to read the writing out loud to her. I wanted to say, *Don't we know each other from when we were just babies?*

"I am sofa king we todded," I said. She opened her mouth and closed her eyes to laugh but just plonked her head down on her arms. It made me want to laugh along, but I knew I wasn't supposed to. Her friends hugged each other and made high-pitched noises. Brian made huh-huh noises but mostly watched the two girls at his end of the bar. Michelle Strout lifted her head off the bar and said, "We todded . . ." in a breathless way. I remembered her grandfather was a milkman back when those still existed. He may have been the last one in the world for all I know. He gave away kittens on Halloween.

I downed the last inch of my beer and Michelle went back to her friends. Brian brought me another beer and took the old one away. I wished I smoked cigarettes still. It's easier to do nothing by yourself when you smoke.

By and by more people started coming through the door and clouds covered over what was left of the sun and made it dark, making the Royal Oak seem more like a night-time place. The jukebox played The Rolling Stones' "Harlem Shuffle." Nobody I could call my friend seemed to come in. I peeled the label off my beer and rolled it up into a tight tube, folded it over a couple of times, unfolded it, put it in the ash tray.

I made my way over to the bathroom and squeezed past a pair of guys throwing darts into the dart machine. It made an excited electrical sound as a dart connected. I was alone in the bathroom so I counted what was left of the money I'd brought—there was plenty—and looked myself over in the mirror. I didn't feel too drunk, but knew I must be a little because my reflection started making tough-guy faces at me, which is usually a reliable sign. I don't do that much when I'm acting myself. There was still some grime on my forearms that might be confused with a tan if you were looking from a distance. I ran water over them and dried off with paper towels before going back out past the dart hurlers toward the bar.

Michelle Strout was by the jukebox now, studying the titles in a squinty way that suggested she ought to be wearing glasses but thought she looked better without them. I couldn't remember if she wore them when we were in school. I went over and stood next to her while she punched in some numbers and lowered her head back to the glass to find another tune. I stood there for a little bit before she looked up and smiled and said, "Hey! I wondered where you went to."

"I was at the bar mostly," I said, poking over toward my seat with my elbow. She kept looking right at me.

"You wanna sit down?"

"Sure I do. Let me get my beer. You need one?" She held up a milky drink with ice cubes and a straw in it and shook her head 'no' along with Creedence Clearwater Revival. I snaked through the people standing around. There was a pretty good crowd by then, some people still wearing work clothes, others clean and in new shirts because they'd gone home first. I didn't see Michelle's friends anywhere. There were a couple of college boys sitting at the bar talking to Brian, watching the ball game. They all had their heads craned up sideways to see the television. Brian was leaning on his arm against the bar. I could see his belly pushing out on his T-shirt and felt at my own chub with my hands, stood up straighter.

When he turned his head toward me, I nodded. He plucked one out of the cooler and set it down without moving his feet, held his hand out for my bills. I gave him three and he went back to looking up at the television with my money is his hand.

Michelle was still staring down at the jukebox. She was wearing white sneakers and was kind of kicking one against the floor in a gawky toe-heel-side pattern that took up a fair amount of room. I kept my distance as I came around alongside of her. She whipped her head around at me and was smiling again. Her eyes looked a little sleepy. "You have a car?"

"Yes I do," I said. "It's the old police cruiser."

She looked up at the ceiling and sucked in her cheeks for a second, "You wanna just go out of here?" She was still whacking her white sneaker around on the floor like, 1-2-3, 1-2-3.

"What is that?" I said, indicating at her foot with my bottle.

"I was with Up With People for three years," she said. "I'm just back visiting."

I nodded and said "All right," and walked toward the door keeping people between me and Brian so he wouldn't see me slinking off out of the Royal Oak with a mostly-full Budweiser pressed against my hip.

It had started to rain a little and the concrete walkway that led around to the dirt lot behind the bar held water because somebody didn't account for drainage. A couple slinky worms had worked their way onto the path. We were both careful to step over them. The parking lot, however, was altogether crawling with worms from under the ground. Some real snakesized ones, too. Michelle saw them and said, "Poor little worms."

She bent down to inspect one and made like she was going to touch it, but then stood up quick and waved her hands around and did a quick little tip-toe spritely hopping dance over to the passenger side of my car. I got in first and swept the lunch bags and soda cans off the other side of the seat, transferred them to the back along with my hammer and prybars. There were waxy paper cups with thick straws from the gas station soda fountain on the floor. God, what a mess! I got rid of those too and shoved the door open from the inside. I'd left my own window open when I'd gone into the bar and there was a little puddle on my side of the seat which had soaked into the knee of my jeans while I was cleaning up. I didn't notice it until she got in and I turned around to sit down.

"I remember this car. It was the first one of these I saw. My dad said it was kind of in-betweeny. He'd see it parked at school when he dropped me off and say, 'There's that in-betweeny.'"

"It's a pretty good car. Well-maintained."

She was shoving her fingertips into the dashboard, checking to see if it was hard or squishy. I could see her hands in the light from the walkway lamps. The nails were painted pink and glittery and there was a peculiar bubble ring on her middle finger like a tiny little snow-globe. "They make these cop cars faster than other cars? For—" She let out a yawn and tried to speak through it before covering her mouth with her hand. "Whew. Excuse me. For chases?"

The embarrassing fact is, I mostly drive slow. "Yeah, they might. Hard saying." You didn't need a key to start it up, but I used one anyway. "It's a pretty good car."

I pulled out onto Route 10 and started back out of town and she didn't make any objection. I kind of freeze up at times like that. Some people may just know what to do and say, but I'm not one of them. "The reason I don't play the radio is there's a problem in the electrical and you can hear the wipers through the speakers," I said.

She kind of leaned her head over on her shoulder and said, "Mmmm."

There weren't any cars out on the road and I was glad. I felt a little sneaky driving through the night with Michelle Strout, who I hadn't even seen in something like fifteen years. More than half-a-lifetime. Here was someone Odessa hadn't even ever heard of.

"What's that ring on your finger?"

Her eyes were closed by then. She was kind of purring, maybe humming a song. "Mustard seed," she said and raised up her hand, shook it a little bit so I could hear the hard little seed rattle around inside its plastic case. "I got it in Atlanta. Have you been to Atlanta ever? They have a couple there who run a clown ministry. People are crazy about it. Kids are crazy about it. They have balloons they make things out of."

I didn't say anything back. She looked like she might already be asleep.

"They might have been from Little Rock originally, I forget." She flopped her head over to the other shoulder and then back again. "I never thought anything about Jesus until I got out of here. There's so much to know and there are a lot of people all wrong."

I turned off Route 10 and we wound down to the River Road, bumped up onto the bridge. North of there, the frost heaves of winter had made craters in Route 10 that they'd filled in hastily with soft tar, but those places had slumped and become a new variety of nuisance. The Vermont side, Route 5, was better. It was a smoother trip if you crossed over the river and then switched back farther up. If they were to blindfold you and plop you down in a car with old shocks, you could tell whether you were in Vermont or New Hampshire right off. The Connecticut was a dark and wide canyon underneath us and I drove slowly over the bridge to see the still water below. There were train tracks on the Vermont bank, but trains didn't follow that line anymore. There was a place a few miles south where the bank had washed away. The crossties had fallen into the river and there were just two rails spanning across the place where the bank used to be. It's the sort of thing that would attract teenage drinkers without fear of falling, but there's no good place to park right there and it wouldn't be worth taking the trouble to walk there.

I wanted to ask Michelle if she'd ever jumped off the bridge into the river like we used to do, but she was asleep with her head practically turned around backward on her shoulder like how a duck sleeps. She had her arm wrapped around her body with the little bubble ring and its knuckle in her mouth. I realized I'd stopped the car in the middle of the bridge and that the only noise was the windshield wipers slopping back and forth and the sound of the small motor that drove them. It sounded like a voice saying, "Maw maw . . . maw maw. . . ." I shut them off and then turned the key and the motor revved down. The raindrops tapped on the roof and I tried to make out rain circles down on the river, but it was too dark and too far away. I rolled down the window and heard the wind blowing and the ticking of the steel bridge. I thought about O.D.'s books in their boxes on the TV table and how there were still three cans of Cott cranberry soda that she'd left behind in the refrigerator. I wondered where Michelle's friends from the bar had got to, where we were supposed to be going.

When the rain kind of swelled up and fell harder against the roof for minute, it was like one of those times when a revelation is stuck in your brain all along and then just falls forward so you can see it plainly. Like that, I came to realize I'd forgotten to drape the lumber tarps over the ancient floorboards back at my uncle's place. I imagined the thirsty wood drinking in the rainwater, twisting up in every direction, spoiling.

Michelle let out a noise that was half sigh/half groan

but didn't sound altogether unhappy. With the dashboard lights off, I could barely see her. I reached out my hand and felt for her elbow—the part of her that was pointing at me the most. I found it. It was sharp and bony. The fabric of her shirt was ribbed like wintertime long-underwear. She could have been anybody in the world right then.

"Michelle?" I said. I thought my voice sounded silly by itself in the dark with the wind going by outside. A spray of rain tickled my neck. "Michelle, I need to go somewhere."

She didn't make any noise at all when I started the motor up and backed over the expansion joint of the bridge into New Hampshire. I took the River Road north until it dumped us out onto 10 again. Then I cut back south and drove past where the drive-in used to be a long time ago. There were trees ten feet tall in the long grass where the rows of window-mount speakers once stood. I saw *Star Wars* and *The Rescuers* cartoon movie right there. *Last Flight of Noah's Ark*. The screen remained for years but that was gone now too. It looked like any old field you might see around here. You would never know.

We passed H. Sargeant & Sons Excavating and I saw

the old dead trucks shoved up into the trees behind the shop. They'd rust away sometime in the next million years. The big crawlers and backhoes were here and there, some up on trailers. There was a lit window high up on the side of the corrugated steel wall of the shop and I knew Kevin Sargeant was probably in there sand-blasting, putting new teeth on his father's Kobelco excavator, watching the television, throwing a Nerf ball for his beagle-border collie mix, maybe having a cold beer. He was married now. I bet he remembered Michelle Strout.

The rain had stopped without my noticing and the windshield wipers started to scrape dry over the glass, streaking it with clouds that were hard to see through. The radio isn't mounted to the dash, but just sits in a cavity where some police apparatus used to be. Somebody made a mess of the wiring. With the wipers off, I clicked the radio on low and heard "OOOOOh-oooh, the Israelites. . . ." I turned onto the Hogreeve Road and followed that to Whipple Hill.

My uncle's yellow house looked a mess even in the dark. I'd torn down dividing walls to get at the floor-boards and thrown all the debris out the holes where windows had been. Chunks of plaster and old studs were caught up against the house and in the overgrown yard. The tarps that should have been covering the floorboards were blowing around a little bit, but were kept in the yard by the tire I'd used to anchor them down. I drove by slowly and then pulled into the driveway. Michelle had slumped far down into her seat and I wasn't sure if I should wake her. What was I doing with her anyway? It probably wasn't even midnight yet. I reached over and held her cheek in my hand, but that seemed too personal so I shook her shoulder lightly. She lifted her head up and her hair was in her face, that ring still in her mouth. She kind of looked around a little and then sat up straight.

"What the fuck is this? What is this?" She started groping for the door handle but couldn't find it. I started to reach out for her but got nervous and held my hands up like somebody had said , "Reach for the sky!"

She left off trying to find the handle and plopped herself back against the seat with her head down in her hands. "Fuckin-A," she said.

"I've just got to do something quick here, then I'll take you where you want to go."

"I don't care," she said, but she wasn't talking to me.

I started to open my door and the overhead light blinked on, so I shut it again. "You want to come see?" She waved the back of her hand at me. I couldn't see her face through her hair. I had to reach past her to get the flashlight out of the glove compartment and I worried that she'd think I was trying something, but she didn't acknowledge my actions whatsoever.

The air was warm and felt wet with the ghost of rain. Peepers were making their sound from the woods at the edge of the Christmas tree fields and the occasional bull-frog sounded off from the pond across the road. That poor house. It could have been okay if somebody had saved it in time. The porch rails were hanging off at odd angles with rusted nails poking out from the ends of the busted balusters. I knew without looking that the porch floor was rotted and had weak spots you could fall through. The sliding door that led into the kitchen was all wrong for the place. My uncle did that to his own house and then left for Florida. The ground made sounds under my boots as I walked around the house to the trailer and I wondered if the leather would soak through and wet my feet.

The floorboards were as I'd left them, cinched down under the yellow load straps. I ran my fingers along the edge of the top board and felt where the straps had dug in and made depressions in the wood, but I couldn't tell if I'd just ratcheted them too tight or if the rain had made them go soft somehow. These were the old kind of boards with straight saw lines along the edges—some hardworking horse had to haul them up Whipple Hill from some mill two hundred years ago. I whisked my hand over the top boards and pushed the skim of water away. The rain had made some of the ancient dust gather up into thick spots and I felt them smear across my palm like grease. The coffee can full of old nails was soupy with rain so I tipped it up to let the water drain out through my fingers. Flecks of rust and dirt came out too, and I hoped the nails would still be good. People would pay for those. Plenty.

The boards didn't seem wrecked or anything, and the sky had turned kind of purpley with some stars out. I didn't suppose it would rain again before the sun came up. I laid some of the old studs on top of the stack hoping that their weight would keep the floorboards from twisting, but I knew the damage was done. The tarps were all wet so there was no point in putting those to use. I walked over to the edge of the dogwood that had grown up out of the bank behind the house to relieve myself, and when I turned around again, there was Michelle standing by the trailer looking out at the pond across the road. I killed the flashlight. She heard me coming and turned around with her hands in her pockets and her shoulders shrugged like she was cold.

"This place is so depressing to me," she said. "I turn into a baby again when I come back here. I wish I'd stayed gone."

"You don't miss it?"

"No I do not."

I plucked at one of the straps over the load. It was solid. Maybe I ratcheted it too tight.

"Nobody here knows anything about me. I don't even know how to ride a bike."

I looked up to see if she was looking at me and was surprised to find that she was. The peepers were so loud. They sounded like there couldn't be enough room in the world to hold them all.

"How many years did we go to school together? 'Til we were fourteen? You didn't know I didn't know how to ride a bike that whole time." She said it like an accusation. "Nobody did. You don't think that would come up? Nobody knows what my house was like."

"Your parents don't live here anymore?"

"They live over in Orford. Orfordville. That's where I'm supposed to be right now. I'll catch hell."

I made a smile and said, "You're grown up."

She gave her head a little irritated shake. "Can't you see I'm here on disciplinary measures? Life's not so easy all the time."

I felt like I didn't know where I was. The house was different that time of night and I might as well have not spent a single minute there before, it felt so unfamiliar standing in the yard with Michelle. "Do you mean you were locked up?" Normally I would have had trouble asking something like that, but I was starting to not feel much like myself. She just shook her head and turned back toward the pond. It looked like a silver circle out in the field. I said, "I got locked up once, but they told me it was mostly to keep me from hurting myself. It was kind of bullshit. I had a girlfriend who used to fight with me a lot. Just shouting, I mean. A statey picked me up walking down the road in the dark. She called 911 and said I might hurt myself, so they had a guy out looking for me. I was just walking down the road. But it was winter and I probably would have froze, so I guess it was good they found me now that I look back on it."

"Haven't you ever wanted to go live somewhere else besides here?"

There were butternuts on the ground and I toed at one in the dark. You don't see butternuts much anymore.

"I used to be petrified about that idea." I didn't say that I'd been to places like San Diego once and Florida twice or all over Maine and Massachusetts for one reason or another. "But now I think I like it here except sometimes it seems like there's nobody I know around."

"You seemed like smart enough kid. I would have thought you'd be long gone and I'd be the one still home." I could barely remember being in school with her. I remembered she had a blue sweater with pink squirrels across the front. It made me feel old talking to her then. I felt like a long time had passed. She walked over to me, leaned against the stack of floorboards and said, "You probably weren't figuring on hearing all my problems." I knew this was the time I was supposed to kiss her or let her know she could kiss me. I'd wanted to earlier, but right then I felt like I wanted to be at home for a change and wanted Odessa to call. Because I was pissed at her and I missed her.

"Sorry if I embarrassed you before. I didn't know it was you and we were laughing about that retard trick."

"I don't mind. Sometimes I am retarded."

I kissed her anyway, because it seemed unavoidable, but in kind of a half-assed way on the side of her mouth that ended up seeming more like I was consoling her for some kind of loss than trying to make fire fly from my mouth. Her lips seemed small and I wondered how we were going to get away from there.

"Do you want me to drive you out to Orford? You can stay at my place if you want, but it's not much."

She had her thumbs hooked in her pockets and drummed her fingers against her thighs. It was like we hadn't kissed at all. "You have a cigarette?"

"I quit a year ago."

"You don't have a cell phone, do you?"

I shook my head. Even if I did, they still don't work around here.

"There's some people I would like to call and tell them I'm just fucking fine." She curled her lips in and stuck out her jaw in an unbecoming way. "God, why did I come back up here?"

"Let's drive out. I don't like this place in the dark."

"I wouldn't mind just sitting here for a minute," she said. "You don't have to if you don't want to. You can leave me."

I was ready to go. I was feeling tired and dried out from working in the dust early in the day and drinking beer all evening. It was catching up with me and seemed like I could never sleep enough to get back to normal. Michelle slid herself down the sides of the stacked floorboards until she was crouched close to the ground in a way that would have been painful for my own legs. I looked out at the still surface of the pond across the road. It was a firepond. Someone had dug it a long time ago. There were cattails grown up all around it and invisible frogs that made noises all night. I stood there for a minute and then said, "Well, I suppose," and walked back to my car.

I wished the seat reclined. But for some police reason, it didn't. I laid my head back on the headrest and tried to fall asleep, but the house in front of me looked more sad than sinister now and I thought about it being pushed down by Haro Sargeant's backhoe and trucked away like rubble to get thrown into a landfill. After a while the passenger door opened and the light came on and I woke up from sleep I didn't even realize I was having. Michelle said, "Okay," and sniffled through a stuffed-up nose that showed she'd been crying out there in the wet grass.

"Your folks' house?"

She nodded a bunch of times, little nods, quickly like she was trying to hold back tears with only moderate success. I backed out of the driveway and drove back down Whipple Hill.

The trees you see when you drive these roads are tall and skinny. There are pieces of stone walls from when this was all cut down and made into a kind of sheep world. There have been a thousand people who don't live here anymore. At night you can see patches of white birch only. Up high, there are spruces. Cottonwoods on the river. Alders along the brooks. Different kinds of maple plus sometimes box elder. There are purple and green stripes of tubing that carry sap from sugar maple to plastic tank. They stay up all year. You can see where the snowplow gouges trees that are too close to the road, and you can see where the dirt roads have sunk over the years so that there are high mossy banks on either side with roots sticking out, dead in the air over the ditches. There are abandoned cars old enough to be surrounded by good sized trees and far enough into the woods that you might not see them rusting there, away from the road. There are cellarholes in places nowhere near where anybody lives now.

A green and gold New Hampshire State Police cruiser was idling in Michelle's parents' driveway. The house was an A-frame tucked into the trees just before you reach Route 25, with decorative trim running down the roofline from ridge to rafter tail. There were lights on in the house and the whole front end was lit up. I cut the headlights and eased in next to the cruiser and heard a woman's robot voice clipping in and out, speaking numbers over the radio. Michelle was staring down at her hands.

She looked up at me, calm. "I'm sorry to make you part of this."

The porch door opened and Edna Strout stepped halfway out, holding onto the doorframe. I could see Charles Strout wearing his green work clothes through the glass front of the house, a hatless state trooper next to him. They were looking out at me and Michelle, sitting there in the dark, looking back at them.

"You can have this," she said, and gave me her little glass bubble ring with the mustard seed inside. "Free of charge. I've got a box full. I'm sorry again."

She opened the door and got out, walked up the driveway passing the trooper who was walking down. He stopped and turned his whole body around like someone with a sore neck does and stared after her. I could see where her pants were dirty and wet from sitting in my uncle's yard. She went up onto the porch and past her mother and across the front windows out of sight. I couldn't see her father anywhere.

I started to open the door to get out, but the state trooper held the palm of his left hand out in a way that said, *Stay inside*. He walked past my window and then turned around and leaned forward so his head was level with mine. The radio on his belt chirped in sync with the one in his car.

"Had much to drink tonight?" His accent was from somewhere else.

"Not much." He stood and ran a flashlight over the side of my car, through the back windows.

"Did she harm you in any way?"

"No, sir."

"Is she harmed?"

"No."

"Her parents know where to find you if I have to ask you anything else."

"I believe so. I live nearby."

"Okay then." He walked back up the driveway and into the house.

I backed out onto the road and turned my headlights on. The road bent up and around the rise in front of me. I blinked my eyes and started for home.

INDIAN SUMMER SUNDAY

IN THE DARKNESS at the edge of the orchard I sat and drank and watched the pickers pit roosters against each other in a blue plastic swimming pool. It's the kind of cheap pool you see all over the place, on lawns and porches all summer long. There were maybe two dozen men standing around in a circle trying to keep quiet, just sort of chanting in Spanish and English and languages of their own. But they'd been drinking too, and couldn't keep from crying out every now and again. Most of what I heard was the flapping of wings and the *skitch skitch* of talons on plastic. By the number of men in the circle I figured some of the Jamaican pickers from the other orchards nearby had found their way over to the Mexicans' territory.

It was almost four in the morning on a Sunday and I had until ten o'clock to clear my head. But I'd come to where I was not welcome in the middle of the night to hide in a hedgerow and watch these workers fight roosters for each other's money. The sun wasn't even up yet, but it was still hot as noon. My beer was warm. I was holding off on that for the time being and concentrating on what was left of the gin.

They had five cars around the other side of the pool with headlights on. I just saw silhouettes.

It's hard to say just how drunk I was. Hiding in undergrowth watching a bunch of strangers fight roosters just before daybreak is a rather uncertain reality anyway, so who knows? Things always seemed fairly unclear when I was drinking.

There was a lot of murmuring as a fight ended, dollars being passed around. A figure stepped out from the circle and walked toward me with a black rooster under his arm like a football. His other hand covered the bird's head. He stopped fifteen feet off from the trees where I lay and got down on one knee. He could have seen me if he'd known where to look, and I could see that he was not a Mexican at all, but a white hippie kid with knots of hair and no shirt. His beard grew thin where it came up over his mouth. The rooster was purring and sounded like its throat was clogged. Even I could tell that it was close to death.

He pulled a bottle of something from the pocket of his

shorts and poured it here and there on the rooster's body, rubbing it in and talking to himself—or to the rooster, it was hard to tell. He was trying to save it, and it was making long low sounds as though moaning to be saved. Behind him, the next fight was already underway and a short man was poking into the pool with a stick to goad the roosters into action. I heard the hippie speak to the bird in a loud angry whisper, like a private fight between two men, "*Bitch!*" It sounded so close, my skin moved, and I knew I was about to witness violence. Quick, he whipped the rooster up by its neck and brought it back down again, two-handed like a pickaxe. He spat at it, throwing his hands up and turning back to the circle of men. He walked a few steps before coming back and kicking the rooster across the grass to near where I hid. Then he hurled the bottle of salve after it, into the trees over my head. I heard it bump down through the branches.

After the Mexicans had walked down the road and the Jamaicans disappeared in their car, it was quiet and dark and I felt very much alone lying there in the branches and dirt. I finished off the gin and picked up the big black rooster. I couldn't see to just leaving it there for the vultures and flies when moments before it was alive and fighting for life. Its neck was thick and soft except for the places where blood had thickened to paste. I could smell an antiseptic fruitiness from where they'd spat brandy under its tail feathers to make it crazy for fighting. Its skinny tongue drooped out of its mouth and I shook its head to keep it from licking my hand.

I walked like that, a heavy dead rooster in one hand and four twelve-ounce cans of warm beer in their plastic retainer in the other, back to my Buick, hidden at the edge of the woods.

With the headlights off, I drove slowly by the light of the moon between rows and rows of twisty apple trees, looking for the way out of the orchard. The air was thick with the heat and the sweet smell of soft fruit rotting into the ground. I still had six hours until I was due before the congregation and I turned on the radio to see if a radio crusader could provide me with a way in. But there was only an all-night call-in talk show, coming in loud and clear from someplace far away. And by the time I found my way to the orchard gate, there was a woman calling from Norristown, Pennsylvania, saying with complete conviction that Arabs are descended from virgins raped by devils. As if she were there. As if she knew the truth of all the cosmos and history.

INDIAN SUMMER SUNDAY

The road led me over bumps and holes and eventually past the pickers' barracks where a few cars sat on the dirt yard between the long cinderblock buildings. Four young women were out leaning on the hood of a small Chevrolet, trying to make Saturday night last. They had a candle in a soup can and fans of playing cards between them. Sunday is the day they rest. I held the steering wheel in both palms and whispered through the windshield as I passed them by, "When the liquor wears you down, you *will* rest." Saturday night will always lead to Sunday morning. Their heads turned to watch me pass and it unsettled me to be seen. I drove a little faster.

I'd taken to driving up there Saturday nights. It's a different kingdom altogether, but it doesn't last. There's no disappearing.

Farther down the road, two Mexicans were walking on the grass strip between tire ruts. They were drunk, I could tell by the heavy way they walked. I was practically on top of them when they heard me and turned around. They just stared dumb, so I flashed the lights and they squinted like jacked deer. One was fat and the other skinny, just like a joke you might tell. There's no way they could have made it back to any of the other orchards on foot without waking up in a ditch first.

"Need a ride?" I said to the fat one, who stood on my side of the road. His eyes were half closed and he wore a t-shirt with a Death's head decal that said Mess With The Best Die Like The Rest. I didn't have to read it to know what it said.

He didn't say anything, but came back to the door behind me and got in. He sat hard and fell over onto his side mumbling sounds like words. The skinny one seemed a little less enthusiastic but got in next to me and leaned against the door. Neither of them said a word. They smelled of wood smoke and peppermint liquor. I turned my on lights and drove down the road.

The skinny one looked at me and then away again, out the window. "English?" I said. He looked at me again, his swimming eyes seeing right through me. He didn't even know where he was. The fat one snored in the back seat.

I reached for a beer where I'd put them, half-under the seat, and felt the greasy wingfeathers of the dead rooster there. Their touch surprised me and felt like electricity in my fingertips. I found the beer and when I offered one to the skinny Mexican next to me, he took it and I tried to stuff the body of the rooster beneath the seat with my heel while he fussed over the beer can. He was having trouble getting his thumb under the tab. I was having trouble getting the rooster further out of the way. I quit trying. It wasn't his bird anyway.

The dirt road turned to pavement with a bump and we passed by a few dark trailers, pick-up trucks in the driveways, empty *Union Leader* boxes glowing bright orange in my headlights.

Out on the highway I drove the Buick south, towards Lebanon. I guessed they'd made their way north from the Bouchard orchards. It was as good a guess as any. The only lights on the highway came from semis driving north, from Boston or Hartford or New York, Baltimore, Atlanta, Miami. Soon the skinny Mexican was asleep too, the can of beer between his legs. With his head tipped back, I imagined I could see buck teeth and desperado mustache.

I took the Lebanon exit and pulled into the huge over-lit parking lot of the Grand Union supermarket that went up the year before or the year before that. I left the car in the fire lane and went inside. There were girls in red aprons sitting on the checkout counters and they looked over at me as the electronic door squeaked open to let me into the light. They looked too young to be working the night shift during the school year and it made me get lost in the seasons for a minute. In the aisles, men my age were shelving boxes of cereal, relish, spaghetti from rolling carts. I was the only customer in the brilliant, enormous place. My knees were tired and the insulated steel beams of the ceiling were a highway in the sky. The fluorescent lights pained my eyes as I gazed upward and I had to shut them for a minute. My feet lead me to the beer and wine section where I carefully withdrew two six-packs of Genesse one at a time. I carried them through the canyons of paper towel, bright bottles of detergent, toothpaste, cough medicine until I reached the register and asked the girl what time it was. She pressed a button on her cash register which made 5.12 flash on the little screen. They aren't supposed to resume selling until six o'clock but she took my money anyway and I knew there wouldn't be any change. My feet took me to the automatic doors.

I'd been drinking for almost three weeks by then. I'd lost my appetite for anything other than white bread, dry noodles, sometimes a potato. My body yearned for them at times, asking for something to soak up the poison pouring through my liver. The congregation had become foreign to me and I wanted to slip away without harm but there was no direction to turn except inward. The new people seem to come in legions until it seemed there was no more room in the little church. I couldn't speak a word to them from my heart. What is worse than having to speak with a false heart? I don't know that drinking helped any, but it's the route I found. It was new to me, at first. I tried it on like a hat I knew wouldn't fit right.

Outside, I saw that my skinny passenger was busy puking in the parking lot. He was hunched over in a desperate three-point stance like a palsied football player, coughing and spitting. I got to my door and saw that he'd left a thin trail of vomit on the seat as well, but I was too tired to care much. The fat one was dead asleep. I put the beer on the roof of the car and opened the back door. In the light, I could see that he wasn't fat so much as muscular like a railworker: thick through the middle. He was wearing green running shoes with untied laces. I shoved at his feet and said, "Time to wake up." He sort of shook his head and worked his mouth, so I knew he was on the verge of coming out of it. I reached over his chest and yanked on his ear the way my father did to me and his eyes opened up a little. The skinny one was sitting over on the curb, head in his hands, and the big one plopped down beside him. The buzz from the orange tungsten lights high above the parking lot was everywhere. I looked up to see millions of insects flying circles around the lightbulbs, dumb bugs with no better use for themselves.

"*Vaya con Dios*," I said, getting back into my car, like in the song. I may be wrong, but I could swear they both said it back to me, "*Vaya con Dios*."

Back on the highway, going north this time, I rolled the window down to get some cool fresh air. I pried the bottle cap off with the seatbelt and slid the six-packs back behind the passenger seat and felt the power of the Buick seep through my arms and legs—a soft bulwark between here and what lies ahead. On the radio was Good Times and Great Oldies Guaranteed Ten in a Row, "Stagger Lee" by Lloyd Price. I dropped the empty into the cardboard carrier and braced the steering wheel against the turn signal lever with my pinkie to make sure I drove straight and true. The radio signal began to fade as the highway crept closer to the mountains.

Turning the knob revealed only low Quebecois voices coming down from Canada early in the morning.

Before long, it was dawn, and beautiful. With the windows down it was cool at least, and smelled a lot less like vomit. The clock on the dashboard said quarter to seven. I knew I'd been sleepwalking in front of them all. It was the effect I'd aimed for, letting words spill out automatically. I was trying to break through to whatever might come next. I had tried to be a friend to anybody, but it seemed to matter less and less whether I was there at all. To the early sunlight coming at me through the windshield, I said "Not everyone that saith unto me, Lord, Lord, shall enter the kingdom of heaven." It sounded like an accusation more than a warning, and I knew it had been a lifetime since learning the words.

In those days of early autumn the church was crowded no matter what I said. I addressed a congregation of strangers, of newcomers, of transients and settlers. At times it looked like ants and insects swarming over the pews and I was bewildered by what I saw. Those who had elected me to this place had long since died off or receded into the shadows.

The sun was hard on my eyes. The Buick was low on

gas. I took the next exit and tasted the sourness of my throat and tried to wash it down with beer. I couldn't think to remember the lifetime gone by.

I saw the new Cumberland Farms gas station up ahead and drove through a stop sign to get there. I left my car at the curb and when I was nearly to the door, I saw that there were three little kids sleeping under a patch-work blanket in the back of a wood-paneled Aspen station wagon. They looked peaceful in there, packed together with duffel bags and suitcases all around them, seemingly immune to the heat. A little boy was sucking his thumb. I put my hands against the dusty rear window and laid my forehead there too. The glass was hot already and I knew it would be a day without mercy.

I heard the electronic chime of the store's door and looked up to see two men come out, one after the other. One had a gallon jug of dull orangey juice and a box of doughnuts. The other one had a quart of Quaker State. They looked tired—big purple moons under their eyes. They noticed me standing there and regarded me in an unfriendly way.

"Help you with something?" one said in a way that meant, really, *I'd be happy to kick your ass right now*. He reached through the open window to set down his quart of oil and took a few steps toward me.

I tried to say some words, I'm not sure exactly which ones, but all that came out was a dry sound from my throat. I feared he might come bump chests with me. He looked like the sort who might do that right before catching you in the ear with a heavy straight-arm kind of punch, and it seemed that his brain was already set to throw one. But the other man was back in the driver's seat by then and the one looking at me seemed to judge me not-worth-it and got into the car himself. They backed out and I tried so much not to look at them that I couldn't help but blink hard until water came out of my eyes.

Inside the store, Dwight Pike was in a white t-shirt and brown elastic suspenders, leaning on his knuckles against the counter and not talking to his big wife, Joann, who stood behind it. They looked at me when I came in and he nodded meaningfully. It was cool in the store, but I got two little packages of Fig Newtons from the display at the end of the aisle and paid for them and left as fast as I could, forgetting about gas, with the heat of their eyes on my back.

I could promise that the sun had grown twice as bright while I was inside. The heat from the asphalt felt like it was wafting up my pant legs and making my knees swim. The Fig Newtons felt like they were getting softer by the second in my damp hands. I was dying from the inside-out right there. I didn't even know why I'd bought the cookies.

When I opened the car door, I saw two empty beer cans and the rooster stuffed under the seat. Its tongue was hanging out onto the accordion-shaped shroud at the gearshift's base, gray and black. The deathly sights and smells of my car hit me like a fist and I gagged but didn't throw up, though it was close in my throat for a minute. My saliva was ropy and I had to spit it out onto the asphalt where it darkened into little black spots. The car wanted to be abandoned forever but there was no place to walk to.

I held my breath and got off the lot and up to speed as quickly as I could without spinning my tires, heading west toward town. I couldn't stand to look at the rooster any more—I wanted to get him out of my awful car and into the ground. The need for it flashed around my brain like a flying snake. He deserved a proper burial, like any living thing, an event that I could preside over. I pounded the steering wheel and the sky turned blue. I could feel my whole head well up with the fluids that come with tears. The perfect swaying beauty of the tall hydrangea trees on the side of the road as I pulled off the pavement and climbed the rise to the Old Cemetery carrying the wasted body of a black rooster on a hot Indian summer Sunday made me turn inside out.

I drove up through the cemetery toward the top of the hill. There were small American flags at most graves, leftovers from Memorial Day. The sun had bleached their little wooden flagstaffs pale. I saw the acres of granite and marble and trees and was amazed that death had destroyed so many in this little town. There was a recent grave with its pink marble headstone where Vera Whitcomb went into the ground, dead at ninety-seven. How many weeks ago? A thin coat of new grass had been stunted by the dry heat and the sod on her grave had turned yellow.

At the top of the hill, I stopped in the gravel lot and pulled the rooster from his place against the transfer case. The blood had firmed up into little rocks under his feathers. I saw the muscles of his legs and the meaty feet.

There were cutters made from the folded red and white aluminum of a Budweiser can attached to his spurs by loops of thin wire and frayed tape, but they didn't look they could have ever done much damage to anything. His comb had been ripped part-way off his head and I saw the dark patch of dried blood where it had been torn from the short red feathers of his scalp. He wasn't born for fighting. The hippie who left him to die seemed a long way gone.

I got all the way over to the treeline where I meant to lay the rooster and scraped at the ground with my heel, but the heat had sucked all the moisture out of the top-soil and I just loosened crumbles of grass and dirt.

It was cooler within the shade of the trees and I broke through the low branches until I found the clear spot where I laid the rooster out flat on a bed of red pine needles. With my hands, I scraped away the needles and twigs and dug a few inches into the black earth. Not deep, but enough to make a bed for him. I had to search for a while to find the five or six decent stones I used to surround his body. They came up without a fight and left dry craters behind. Then I piled most of the pine nee-dles from the clearing onto the grave so that it became a red lump in the center of a dark earthen circle. My own voice startled me when I heard it in the quiet of the woods as I said what I could remember of the Order for the Burial of the Dead over his grave. I shook some dirt over the mausoleum I'd made and stood there in the woods seeing what I had just completed. It made me proud and joyous to finish the burial and I felt clear-headed and exhausted. When I lay down, my eyelids shut out the world.

THE SOUND of the church bells banging out the hour of ten o'clock woke me. I found my way back out of the woods and walked across the cemetery to the back door of the church with an emptiness in my stomach and the sun burning hot on my head. The members of the choir were already there, in their white robes, their faces talking and smiling as they waited in the shade outside the church. They didn't seem to notice me as I passed through their numbers to reach the door. The organ was loud from inside. I stopped at the top of the stairs and brushed the red needles and dirt from my clothes. From where I stood, I could see my car at the other end of the cemetery, small, its door flung open, its gas tank empty.

Inside, I bumped into bustling bodies as my eyes adjusted to the darkness. The new deacon passed me quickly on his way to the bell tower door. In a few seconds I saw him leap down the stairs with the heavy braided rope in his hands. The bell sounded deep and low. His teeth flashed, and in a moment he was flying back up the stairwell like a goblin, pulled by the weight of the bell. I got into my clothes and peeked out across the transept to where the sound of commingled voices came from packed pews. The young organist from the college conservatory was playing something too tricky. He was showing off.

There was an order of worship bulletin on the table by the door and I read it.

It said, at the top, The Baptismal Christening of Margarita Ruano Fragoso.

At the change of the organ's melody, the choir filed past me into the bright room of the church. I stepped out from the corner and followed them. The pulpit had been varnished since last week and was darker. I fingered it to see if it was as smooth as it looked. It was. I switched on the reading light and looked out into the congregation. There were colors and I had to hold on to the sides of the pulpit to keep balanced.

In the first row, a Mexican couple in dark clothes was smiling up at me with tears in their eyes. The father blinked and thrust a baby girl in a long white dress up above his head, presenting her to me.

—MATTHEW 15:11

HAY PEOPLE

ANOTHER TRUCK WENT BY—a brown one. Junie knew this one. It had a part that clanked when it rolled over the gravel. She'd seen it go up her driveway into the fields yesterday morning and then heard it go down again in the night, making that loud clattering noise as it went. They were here even earlier this morning. The first ones went up while she was still in bed. It had surprised her when she heard a man yell, heard horses' hooves on the gravel below her window. Two big horses by the sound of their steady steps. Their hooves clip-clopped on the driveway while she pulled her blanket up over her chin.

Junie was canning tomatoes in the kitchen when she saw the brown truck roll by. There was a man driving it and a bunch of small dirty children in the back staring right in at her. She pretended not to notice and walked over by the sink to be out of sight, but the truck was already gone.

They were new hay people. She didn't know anything

about them. Before, her brother and his family had done the cutting. But they were gone now, and it didn't look as though they were coming back.

Soon a green station wagon with a lot of loose things tied to its roof went by, going up the hill toward the barn and beyond. The tires on the gravel made a low crunching sound. An old man with a big floppy hat was driving and a fat woman was in the seat next to him. The back seat and trunk were filled with boxes and what looked like fabric—rugs, maybe. The car's body rode low on its wheels.

Jars of tomatoes lined the counter in the kitchen. Soon she would put labels on them with the date. But there was no hurry—not until she canned something else red.

The hay people weren't from town. While hanging a sign to sell off her brother's discarded possessions, Junie had seen a filecard tacked up outside the store. Someone had tried to stay between the pale blue lines with a shaky felt-tip pen. The card had been there for a while and water had gotten to it. The ink had bled a little and a line of rust trailed down from the thumbtack. It said FIELDS CUT + ODD JOBS/other. There was a crossed-out phone number and another written in pencil.

When Junie called, a young voice answered and she

couldn't tell whether it was a boy or a girl. She asked could she speak to either the father or the mother but heard someone take the phone from the child before she could finish. The new voice was older—an adult voice. It must have been the mother of the child. Or maybe a baby-sitter?

"I was calling about the haying. I saw a sign?" she said.

"Well, we just tell them when they get a job. They don't have a phone. I can tell them if you want."

Junie didn't know what to say so she said thank you, she'd call again and hung up immediately. The fields kept growing and a week later she called back. At first she tried to speak with a different voice, but she slipped from it and told the woman on the other end that she needed her two big fields cut and the bales put up. She explained where she lived. The other woman said okay, she'd tell them.

The next day, a young man with yellow hair like the hair on a dog's belly came to her house. She'd been in the bathroom when she heard him knock and was startled and embarrassed. By the time she looked up and saw that it was an unfamiliar face looking through the screen door, she was halfway across the living room floor. She wiped her hands on her shirt for no reason.

"You called about your fields?" he said, looking at her chin, or her neck. He was young, twenty-five or so. Younger than her brother's son. She said yes and he asked if he could see them. She pointed up beyond the barn to where the driveway passed under the first gate and became two ruts in the grass. He nodded and walked away toward the barn. She watched him through the screen door and saw that he had red mud on his boots and spots of it on his bluejeans.

When he came back hours later, she was in the barn getting eggs. She didn't like the chickens. They'd belonged to her brother and he hadn't even bothered to mention them when he said he was going. She hated the way they fluttered and ran past her on both sides when she entered the coop and then did it again when she was leaving. She hated the feel of the small eggs when they were warm and rough and surrounded with little gray feathers. She'd give the birds away before slaughtering them herself.

The young man came into the barn while she was gathering the eggs into the fold of her shirt. When she heard the sound of his boots echoing on the floorboards, she hurried to put all the eggs on the wooden shelf. One rolled off and landed in the hay but didn't break. He was outside the coop door, waiting. She didn't like his way of standing. It looked as if he might not hesitate to reach out at her.

He said they'd do it and gave her a price. Junie said that sounded reasonable and wiped her hands on the tails of her shirt. He said he'd be back in a few days with his family and they'd do the cutting. When he looked down at her feet, she looked down too and saw that a black rooster had come out from behind her and she realized she'd left the door open. By the time she got the rooster back inside, the young man had already walked down beyond the cottonwood in the dooryard. He passed the house and walked onto the road, going down the hill without looking back.

A WEEK LATER the cars arrived for the first time. Then an old tractor with a baler. Then those horses. That was five days ago, or maybe a week. It was hard to remember. She canned about half the beans and ate some soup from the pot on the stove for lunch. It was summer, but cool. It had been a cool summer all along.

In the evening the horses came down past the house.

Their heads bounced as they walked and she saw how their big muscles twitched under the skin. She tried to remember if she'd seen them come down the night before. Eventually the station wagon came; this time the fat woman was on the side closer to the house. She had her big arm on the ledge of the window and it looked puffy. The skin was sunken and pinched into a flower at the elbow. The brown truck came last and she heard its familiar sound from up above the barn. She heard it coming then heard it stop and go twice, and she knew they were opening and shutting the gate. Then it went by and she saw that it was missing its windshield. The children were in the back and also two dogs. One had whorls of black and brown hair. The other had a long coat and its tongue was hanging out. The two dogs were turning around in the bed of the truck and the children leaned against the sides. A little girl with long straight hair was braiding strands of field grass into a rope. They turned the corner and she heard the clanking of the truck as it disappeared down the hill toward town.

That night Junie built a fire in the woodstove using some of the last logs from the woodshed. She remembered that she'd have to make arrangements for firewood before fall. When was the last time she'd needed a fire this early in the year? That night, she lay in bed thinking of the things that needed doing. Just before light, she thought she heard voices and footsteps going down the driveway, but she wasn't sure.

In the morning, she got up and made coffee. The milk was bad. The greasy feel stayed on her tongue and she had to eat a teaspoon of sugar to get rid of the taste. She made a list of things to get at the store on Sunday. The canning was done so she filled a bucket with vinegar and water and cleaned the counters in the bathroom and the kitchen. Then she rinsed out the bucket and pulled on her coat to go feed the chickens.

Junie was startled to see the brown truck parked next to the barn. She turned quickly and went back inside. She hurried up the stairs and tried to watch out of her bedroom window, but the cottonwood blocked her view. She stayed put and in a while she heard the truck go up and through the gate toward the fields. She busied herself in the house, waiting for the horses and the station wagon, but they never came.

In the middle of the night, she was awakened by the sound of the brown truck coasting down the driveway.

She heard it steer its wheels on the gravel and roll out onto the road and down the hill. After a few seconds, she heard the engine cough as the driver popped the clutch. She tried to remember who drove the brown truck.

ᔕ□□ᴎ, the cars and horses stopped coming down in the evening and she would occasionally notice a child or a couple walking up or down the driveway. Once, she was cleaning out the coop when she heard feet in the hay loft above. They started, walked across the ceiling, and stopped. But the noises she heard at night kept her awake.

Sometimes it was just the sound of voices from far away, up in the fields. Other times she could swear she heard music. Music! Two days went by and she saw no one on the driveway. She collected the eggs without hearing any footsteps from above. But at night the sounds were louder. She heard laughter and singing and, she was sure now, instruments. She strained her ears and sometimes thought it was only winter coming that she heard. She couldn't be sure.

She hadn't been able to sleep. Her stomach felt tight and her skin hurt.

On Wednesday, she sent postcards to the people who had bought hay from her in the past. She gave a price higher than last year's. The weather hadn't been as agreeable. Cold and no rain. She had begun to cough a dry and empty cough that made pain in her ribs.

On Saturday, her knees became weak while she stood on a chair in the kitchen with her arms raised to clean cobwebs from the ceiling corner. She had to sit down on the chair until her vision settled. She spent the rest of the day in bed, alternating between hot and cold. The nights and days became mixed as she slept and woke into a half-sleep. She heard the music and felt small under her heavy blanket. The windows were shut and the world outside seemed dull and distant through the gauze of the curtains. She focused on a knot in the beam above her head and then slept. She saw the knot and heard music and children and the slow voices of old men.

Junie remembered that her mother had told her, "Hay is for horses." She remembered a teacher scolding her for chewing on strips of paper torn from the corners of schoolwork. She remembered eating oranges at Christmas. She slid out of bed and walked through the door with the blanket dragging behind her, past the barn and up the hill. She unlatched the gate and let it swing out on its hinges. The wind pushed at her nightgown and she pulled the blanket around her shoulders. The gate swung in the gusts and squeaked behind her as she walked along one of the ruts. She sometimes heard the music, but the wind pressed at her ear and made a whine. The ruts entered a thicket and the trees were all around her, making the light from the moon into spots on the ground and everywhere. Her nose was cold and she felt it drip. Her feet were bare.

As she came out of the thicket she saw the enormous hills of grass in the clearing there like sleeping mammoths in the dark. The one nearest was losing strands to the wind and some blew into her hair and against her face. She brushed at them with her fingers and felt the bone in her cheek.

The solid mud of the ruts felt cold at her feet and she could follow them in the dark. She scraped her foot on a stone somewhere.

At the top of the rise, she saw the silhouettes of several cars illuminated by a large fire. Bales of hay lay everywhere. Horses were walking slowly, heads bent down to the grass. When the wind was between gusts she heard the music. One horse turned to her. She reached out a hand and it lifted its head, but then leaned forward so she could lay her palm on its dark face. It rolled its eyes and brought its ears back. It snorted and turned away but she was already walking and the horse lowered its head to the ground. She had lost her blanket.

There were more cars than she had imagined, maybe a dozen. She hadn't ever seen most of them. There was a van with a ladder on the back and things wrapped in plastic on its roof. The cars made a circle and she could see the people sitting around the flames in the center. The fire was leaning in the wind and throwing sparks over a Datsun that was parked there.

Junie walked in a slow circle around the cars, the short stubble of the grass poking at her feet. The wind blew and she couldn't tell if it made her cold or warm. The clouds seemed very near.

She drew closer to the cars and when she reached the van, she felt her knees and stomach disappear. She leaned against the flat side of the van and tried to straighten her back against it but her head wanted to loll down. The music was very loud here and she could imagine the old man in his floppy hat playing a fiddle just on the other side of the van from where she now stood. There would be small dirty children holding hands and turning in a circle around the flames. The young man who had come to her door. The coonhound and the long-haired dog chewing on something and licking at each other. There were people sitting on logs wearing heavy coats and singing, she could hear them. They would sing and sing and wouldn't stop. Maybe they'd never stop.

Her head was heavy and she couldn't keep from swinging it from side to side so that it stretched the skin at the back of her neck. She held her elbows and leaned against somebody's van, somebody who was in the field night and day with a beard and hair on his arms, in her fields laughing out loud while somebody else baled grass and others loaded bales onto a hay wagon. He'd be right there on the other side of the circle of cars. She could see them perfectly in her mind. The old man in the floppy hat looked stern, moving stiffly from the waist up, sawing at the instrument pressed against his bicep with his fat wife next to him, leading the songs. She had a scarf around her head to help her against the cold. A young girl with pigtails was crying in the dark at the edge of the circle, not singing.

She felt the inside of her head sway to meet the grass as she fell and her shoulders became weighty and dull as she lay there. It was dark and she realized that it was because her eyes were closed and that she was very calm. The song was comforting—its melody was familiar and plain and far off, like sounds from another room, like the piano she had heard once through a wall somewhere. The wind blew over her body and was warm, she thought that maybe she felt rain drops. The short cut grass made a ring around her body. It pricked at her and separated her from everything else.

SHE WOKE on the couch in her living room. The sun through the windows warmed the ribbed upholstery and her cheek. She opened her eyes and saw the woodstove and the canning rack by the door to the basement. Three unused jars and some red rubber gaskets lay on the floor. She knew that it would be difficult to move her body and so stayed there and continued to look around the room. The mantelpiece with the framed print of a fisherman casting from a rowboat was there. The great sea trunk that had been her grandfather's. Inside there were shelves that came out. There were sweaters and winter things there. Soon it would be time to have fires every day. It would be time to put on storm windows and to shut off the unused rooms, to stuff towels at the doors to keep winter out. She would give the chickens away. She would find someone. She would ask one of the people at the dump or at the store. She could find someone.

She heard the truck come through the gate and down toward the barn. The barn was useless now, as were the gates, without animals, with the chickens almost gone, without her brother and his angry boy. Just a storehouse for hay that would sit there forever.

The truck came down the driveway and jangled to a stop. A man would come to the door, she knew it. The same young man who had stood too close to her at the door of the chicken coop. He would come and look through the panes in the door before knocking. His breath would make a circle of steam there and he'd knock with one knuckle. He'd rub his hands together against the cold and wipe his feet on the stone step in anticipation of being asked in while she wrote out a check to settle the debt. She could hear his boots on the gravel now.

Junie knew that she wouldn't rise to meet him, that she would rest there until she felt her legs. The hay people would wait. The hay itself would wait. She would leave a barn full of stale hay and dust to remind people that she had once been alive.

DEBT

WEEKS WAS UP in the willow, smoking a Camel for a minute. There were two other damaged willows beside the same brook, but they were smaller and the newer boys would handle them before sundown. As Frank's senior man, it was on him to be up in the tree.

Glenn Bushey, who was now the boyfriend of Linda, Weeks's ex-wife, had the tractor. Weeks could see that one of Glenn's eyes was still a little pinched from where he'd hit him with a wild punch a few nights before.

Weeks sat in the Y of the huge winter-naked tree, straddling the damaged side of the fork. His pants and chaps rode up on his thighs and pinched off the blood to his dangling legs. He knew better than to shuffle around trying to get comfortable. That was how saws got dropped—the saw in this case being the big 288 with a thirty-six inch bar. It belonged to the company, not to Weeks. It had cost Frank seven hundred and fifty dollars on credit on the first day of the ice storm. The job was supposed to pay for the saw, the new tractor tires, payroll. He laid the saw across his thighs and took off his gloves one at a time, blew into each for warmth and put them back onto his stiff hands. The saw hopped around on his lap as its motor idled.

He had already wrapped the damaged limb with a choke chain and then dropped the free end down to one of the younger boys. The boy hooked the chain to a steel cable which now cut a tight line through the cold air all the way down to the skid-plate on the back of the blue Ford tractor. To get the right pulling angle, Glenn had pushed the nose of the tractor halfway into the box elder whips at the edge of the woods.

The boys stood in a circle beside the tractor taking turns at breathing in smoke from a brass pipe. Their saws and gas cans and jugs of bar lube were piled together at the base of an undamaged maple. It was the end of the day, gusty, and every so often one of the boys would lean his head down by the hub of the tractor wheel to shield himself from the wind as he passed his lighter over the pipe's bowl. They all had white clouds drifting from their mouths.

Glenn was kneeling on the tractor's seat, awkwardly reaching forward over the steering wheel to fit the cuff of his wet glove around the exhaust pipe. It was the best way to warm your gloves if you didn't mind the smell it left on your hands. Weeks hoped Glenn wasn't still mad. He knew Glenn might not pull the lever to engage the winch if all the younger boys' backs were turned. The saw would get pinched under the weight of the big vertical limb. It would slow them down until after dark and then some of them would have to come back the next day to finish. It would spoil the whole job schedule and Frank would hold it against Weeks, who was supposed to make sure everything ran smoothly. Or the branch could swing back at him where he was trapped if Glenn did his part wrong. But Weeks tried not to think about that possibility. He didn't think his debt went that far.

He finished his cigarette and let it fall through the air to the crusty snow. The wind spun it around and then whisked it over the bank into the brook.

The short warm spell of the previous few days had broken the ice and the water ran quickly now, even at its low winter level. Almost every tree had been damaged in the storm.

Weeks lifted the saw and worked the trigger a few times. The chain whirled. The long bar leaped with each pull. Down by the edge of the woods, Glenn knelt on the tractor seat. Weeks tried to read his face but Glenn was giving him a blank stare to make him guess.

He turned the saw against the big tree limb and leaned close to the chain as it cut into the soft wood of the broken tree. The boys down below turned to watch the sawdust spray across his chaps and float away on the wind. Glenn's hand rested on the winch lever.

Weeks knew in his heart that Glenn and Linda couldn't last. He might even get another chance with her himself, but that wouldn't last either. It was important that they finish the job and move on to the next. "Please," he said, over and over and over again.

FEARLESS WARRIORS

I'M THE HAPPIEST there is in the world," Pepsi said, to nobody more than me, causing a twist of nervousness to settle in my stomach. "Anybody says he's happier than me is just *dying* . . ." His head lolled back as he brought his fists up.

Pepsi was getting married to a girl named Tammy Lesage, which isn't at all an Indian name, though she came down here from an all-Indian town in Maine with the bully who beat her up so much he had to go to North Haverhill. He got out and did it again and now he's in Concord, as is what typically happens to those that prove they deserve it—mean creeps. Pepsi's own marriage to her would end fairly quickly, but in a withering way—without any high drama.

Most of us were just standing around on top of the Royal Oak, watching the fireworks pop up in the dark. Independence Day!

From up on the roof, we could see the explosions of light from two different towns down along the river.

Smoke clouds bled together into fog all down the valley. Our town would launch up a wonderful round burst of light, illuminating the smoke across the river in Vermont. Then they'd return fire. It happens every year. The breeze pushes the clouds south.

The volunteer firemen had left the bar hours earlier to go touch off the rockets they get from down south: North Carolina, South Carolina, someplace. Even as Pepsi was bursting into our peaceful celebration, spitting rum breath at me and the rest, our fire-fighting friends were down on the riverbank lighting fuses and standing around with fire extinguishers. With every airborne explosion, we all thought, in our heads, *There's another one didn't blow the fingers off Don Weeks, thank God.*

Knowing our friends were toying with beautiful explosives had us all squeezing our drinks a little tighter up on the roof, even without the sudden presence of Pepsi, who was raving in his bliss. Who knows what kinds of people they have putting those death-rockets together without any education or anything?

The Royal Oak is just a regular bar now. None of us ever goes there much any more. But it used to be different before kids from the college found it and made it their own. They didn't used to have a fully fledged liquor license. You had to go outside and buy your beer through a window and then carry it back in.

Pepsi's rages were nothing new. I'd known him since kindergarten—which was a long time before he discovered the stultifying effects of drink. You may think that a name like Pepsi is peculiar, but it's not much of a story. I'll tell you that I was called Boss Hogg for a short time, and that I still don't find that very funny. I grew up and got skinnier. My name is not Boss Hogg now. In the seventh grade I saw Pepsi get so mad that he bit a portion of his own index finger right off.

Occasionally one of us gets married and we wish him the sincere best. He might be marrying your sister, and you might know it isn't going to last happily. What else is there to do? Besides, sometimes it endures and, from time to time, prospers.

"I'm happier than you," Pepsi said, poking me hard in the chest with his thumb, "and you," he said, doing the same to Glenn Bushey's arm, causing "The King" to spill a few inches of beer out onto his own pantleg, "and you," he said to Russell Groleau, missing his target entirely and stumbling fully chest-to-chest instead. Russ pushed him back upright onto his feet without really looking at him. He was watching the explosive finale on the horizon.

HELLO!

THINGS GOT BAD FOR ME, but after some weeks went by, they started improving.

My oldest and most favorite animal, a cat named Full Tilt Boogie I'd had since even before meeting Rose, died in the heart of winter. This was almost immediately followed by the departure of Rose to Florida where she said she was relocating. And though I was welcome to join her there, she said, I knew it wasn't really an invitation.

To make matters worse, the General died a final, huffing death and I was stuck with no transportation into town to get groceries or commingle with others. In winter, with snow or cold persuading you to stay indoors, you can get resourceful or you can watch television. I watched television programs about Deadly Swarms and police in Nevada and Oregon chasing drug dealers as they fled on bicycles and in cars. I watched talk shows and award ceremonies for famous people.

Rose carried two cats and one parakeet down to Tallahassee with her. We'd let go of the rabbits a year or so earlier and with dear old F.T.B. buried in the frozen ground, the only person left to keep me company was Gator, a long-tailed feist Rose had found for me at the shelter last summer. But the fellow who'd owned him first treated him poorly, and he kept to whichever part of the house was farthest from me.

I slept for ten, eleven, fourteen hours at a time.

Oprah Winfrey, Montel Williams, Sally Jesse Raphael, *Days of Our Lives*, *One Life to Live*, *ABC Nightly News with Peter Jennings*, *Cops*, Jay Leno and David Letterman.

I saw a wrestler execute his own invention, the "Dutch Hammerlock," time and time again. After midnight, a man sat in front of a map of the universe and said I could buy a star to name after myself or a loved one. On another channel I saw the champion boxer, George Foreman, selling a fat-draining hotdog cooker on national television at two o'clock in the morning.

After two weeks of this, and of living mostly on cans of soup from the back of the cupboard, I caught a ride into town and sold a valuable sixteen-gauge Browning shotgun and some antique bottles that had been my mother's to a fellow I know there. I bought a smoked ham and orange juice and sliced bread and postage stamps and light bulbs and a bunch of rock 'n' roll cassette tapes. I opened a bank account. I went to the bookstore and got a pile of magazines, some in different languages. *Majesty*, *Gun Dog*, *Astronomy*, *Le Monde*, *Der Spiegel*, *Hello!*, *Oggi*. I stopped at the auto supply store to see about parts for the General. The man there offered to buy it off me sight unseen, but I told him no thanks. I carried my grocery bags up to the college and spoke to a professor who, after some discussion, kindly gave me half a dozen phone numbers and lent me a slightly outdated copy of the *Dictionary of Minor Planet Names* by Lutz D. Schmadel. I drank Diet RC in a bar all afternoon and then caught my ride back home, where Gator was whining to get back inside.

With new eyes I saw how unpleasant things had become at home. I had more or less moved out of the bedroom and onto the couch. There were dishes and glasses strewn all around the place and the curtains hadn't been pulled aside in quite a while. I took the TV off the cart and put it into the closet. I threw the blankets in there too and found some others folded up in a chest I hadn't opened in years. They smelled cedary and healthy and I put them on the bed. I turned the pillowcase inside out for the time being.

I checked the mailbox for the first time in a week and there was a letter from Rose saying that the Florida weather was already improving her arthritis and that she'd found a dog grooming place with an open table. With her hands feeling better, she thought she'd take it and try to get a clientele built up.

The next morning I started in making calls. First to the Smithsonian Astrophysical Observatory down in Massachusetts. They told me to call Dean Crocetti, a member of the International Astronomical Union. When I did, he told me a few things and then explained how the Small Bodies Names Committee works. He said he'd been up here on a bicycling vacation. He seemed to like talking to me, I'd say.

We had a warm stretch and most of what was left of the snow turned into sogginess in the dooryard. I fixed a broken rake I found under the porch, pulled all the wet leaves back from around the foundation and piled them up to burn later. The rabbit cage made me half-sad to look at, so I took it apart carefully and put the pieces in the shed. You never know, I might not be through with rabbits forever.

HELLO!

Winter wasn't done yet, but for a couple of days it felt like it.

I called Dean Crocetti again. He remembered me. Doctor Crocetti says that if Earth was a golf ball, Pluto would be a pea eight miles away. And if Pluto's a pea eight miles away, the nearest star, on the outskirts of the Alpha Centauri System, is fifty thousand miles away. Some of what you see when you look out on a winter night are asteroids that are drifting around space forever, passing through our own heavenly realm every now and again. There are one hundred billion stars in our galaxy. He was very kind and invited me, sincerely I believe, to go to Boston and look through the expensive telescopes they have there. I explained that the General was out in the driveway, its tires pretty flat and becoming part of the mud. Besides, I assured him, the stars looked bright and even fairly close when I stood on the steps of my own house and gazed upward.

I took a flashlight down to the basement and found three cans of paint that were still okay. I mixed them together and a decent red color came out of their marriage. I painted the kitchen walls and the floor of the bathroom. I sat at my table and read magazines for the second and third time. I found that if I kind of just skimmed along,

I could even make sense out of the one written in Italian. "Weekend" is spelled the same there as here.

By the middle of March, I got a call from Dean Crocetti saying that the Names Committee had granted approval to the request he'd made on my behalf. Unnamed Heavenly Body #5629, an asteroid on a 4.83-year orbit, officially would bear the name Fulltiltboogie. I could see it in five weeks' time. I told him I was grateful and went to work on my next proposal.

By April, it felt like summer on good days. The green fingers of early flowers were poking up out of the ground. By day I could look up and see buzzards circling in the air. If you forget that they live on dead things and can concentrate on their frozen stillness as they glide (instead of the sad baldness of their tiny red heads), buzzards are beautiful and not entirely ominous.

It's up to the people who discover things in space to give them names. If someone in Belgium and someone in France fight over who saw something first, the International Astronomical Union hashes it out. Usually they'll just credit both people, and a name like "Hale-Bopp" emerges. Many go unnamed, which just proves that we forget how extraordinary some things are if we get too used to them. Dean Crocetti personally is the discoverer of dozens of minor planets, only some of which had names before I first called him on the phone.

#5927: Hellorose; #6328: Gatorthedog.

I STAYED UP all night watching stars blink. It was cold, but I dragged the blankets out to the porch and wore my hat and the snowmobile suit I've had forever. How could I have overlooked all those patterns and important groupings of stars?

The phone rang in the morning and the fellow from the auto parts store said my special order from the factory had come in from Independence, Missouri. He asked a few more questions about the General and again I had to say "no" when he offered me money in exchange for its ownership. No sooner had I hung up with him than Rose called from Florida saying that she too had spent most of the night watching the stars, guessing at which one was named for her.

People are so helpful, I told her. Doctor Dean Crocetti, the man at the college, the people who looked after Gator at the Humane Society, my mother for leaving me those old things to sell for money.

She said I should come down there for a while. Gator and I would benefit from seeing a new part of the country. I said I'd give it some thought, but we both knew I'd be staying where I was. It would be one of those times when I make the wrong choice on purpose.

"I looked at them all," she said, "until I found the one I liked best. It seemed the most like me. I bet that was it."

"I bet so, too," I said. I hoped I was right.

SILVER BELLS

WE WERE WAITING until four o'clock for Western Union to get the money from Clarence, who'd made off with the Mercury and who'd then called two days later full of remorse and good will all the way from Atlantic City, New Jersey. It seemed that he'd had a lucky pull at the slot machines and was going to make it all up to us.

We'd been at the Northstar Motel for the better part of a week by then, waiting for something to spur us along. If you watched carefully, you could see glimpses of pornographic TV between the scrambled lines—some girl's head leaned back openmouthed or maybe some actual skin, but those movies always make me feel worse and it's sort of better to just see little glimpses here and there between the bouncing black and gray lines. Everything else was just Johnny Carson telling the future in a big floppy hat or ads for Christmas records. I'd seen it all a hundred times before and it wasn't any better with the sound turned off.

Matty was faking sleep on the other bed. I say he was

faking because I could see him off the reflection from the TV, lifting his head up now and again to spy me and see if I was doing something he should know about. Things were generally fairly dull.

It was Christmas or maybe Christmas Eve or maybe the day before that. I still had the little Philips transistor radio then and it was playing the music you hear that time of year—"Little Drummer Boy" and "Run, Run, Rudolph." USA for Africa and so on. That little radio. I miss it, for sure. I turned the TV back over to Johnny Carson and watched Ed McMahon mouth the words to something he'd just thought up and make fifty thousand dollars for sitting on the couch in a gray suit on nationwide TV. The remote control was the very old kind—two big buttons sticking up out of a heavy steel case. I pressed the buttons and it let out a wheeze like when you sit down on the cushions of a naugahyde couch in a bus station and all the air tries to escape out.

We'd been living like that for a while, ever since the promise of our reunion with our father in Aurora, Illinois fell apart and his wife said we couldn't stay with her anymore. At odds with each other, we went from one town to the next almost by accident. Clarence, I guess, had reached a tipping point and made off with our Mercury.

I turned up the radio because I knew Matty was awake and just waiting for the day to end so he could go to sleep for the night. On the country station, somebody was doing a Christmas song I remembered from when I was little and our mother was always in the bell choir. They played it every year at the pageant. Matty rolled over so his back was to me and I could see how dirty his socks had become.

We used to have quite a pageant back home in New Hampshire. I got to be a little cherub when we were small and then, when I was a little older, I was a shepherd with some of the other boys. The girls were angels who held onto battery-powered candles that sometimes would conk out right in the middle of one of the songs they were singing. It's like I can see them now, waving those candles around in the dark and singing Gloria! Gloria! and the lights going out. Candles blinking on and off right at the most important time of all: when the girls were supposed to light up the angel of the Lord, come to make the miracle known to everybody. They were all so pretty, despite everything. The pageant was for sure the biggest crowd they ever got in church except maybe for the odd funeral for an old person with a lot of grandchildren and neighbors who knew him for years. It seems like they could have sprung for some new electric candles.

When Matty was a little cherub, he picked the old junker doll they used as the baby Jesus right up out of the cradle. Did he ever get people laughing for that!

I kicked over at his bed. "You remember that time you picked up the baby Jesus doll right out of the cradle?"

He just sort of hunched his shoulders and made a closed-mouth sound. I don't know, maybe he really had fallen asleep by then. After a little bit, he got up and made a big show of stretching and yawning. He wouldn't look at me.

On the radio, the singer was really overworking the poor song like they all will if given half a chance and I listened to the words she was singing about the holly and the green bush. I'd never heard the words before, just bell music. I didn't even know words existed. There was a swell of strings and a bunch of back-up singers came in for the big finish: Hol-ly! Hol-ly! Hol-ly! I used to sing half decent if nobody was around and it was just me and the car radio or whatever. Especially with rock 'n' roll music, which I love. When I was in school I sort of hoped for a while that maybe I'd be one of the wise men from the East when I got a little older and if maybe Don Weeks and Ken Weeks and Russ Groleau got too old for it and quit by then. Seems pretty funny now, I guess. So much water under the bridge.

Don Weeks got to carry the silver jug for myrrh which I always liked pretty well. It seemed like it would be nice to have that crown and fake beard on and everybody knowing it was you underneath, walking down the far aisle with the empty jug of myrrh, singing "We Three Kings" just like last year and just like next year. Everybody listened close when they spoke so well all together, "Where is he that is born King of the Jews?" Everybody listened even if you sang not too well like Russ Groleau did year after year. I remember it all.

By then Ed McMahon was standing up and waving his arms around over his head. Johnny Carson leaned his chin on his hand and looked amused under that big idiot's hat.

Matty came out of the bathroom with a white toothpaste line running down his cheek. He saw me looking at him and felt himself over for a bit before realizing what was wrong. When he went back into the bathroom, I switched the channel back over to the scrambled station. The remote went *wheeze* and then there was a girl in a nurse's uniform on the television. Or maybe she was a sailor. I put my pants on.

My mother played the big heavy bass bells. I can remember seeing her, too. They'd stand in the back, the whole line of women behind the pews with their white gloves on. Even when it was dark as a cave in the church and somebody was singing solo from the balcony, you could see the line of white gloves—hands in palms—waiting patiently. Discipline, they had it.

Me and Matty'd cracked an Alpine stereo out of a Celica in the train station parking lot the night before, so the thighs of my pants were covered in road dust from leaning against the door while I palm-thumped on the window until it let go. The metallic paint on those cars can really hide the dirt. Matty traded the desk man the Alpine for another three days' rent on the room. In Ohio, somebody only gave us one night for a good radio like that. But this was in Pennsylvania, which was new to us.

Those silver bells were plenty heavy, believe it or not.

I don't know what they'd be worth. You need a strong woman like my mom used to be if you expect somebody to keep knocking away at the big ones down on the low end of the musical register. She used to practice in the living room—arrange her set of bells and her gloves and her sheet music and her electric metronome on her ironing board and then she'd do exercises: swinging the bell out from her chest and then muting it back against the towel draped over her shoulder: whole notes, half notes, quarter notes. My brothers Matty and Clarence and me could hear her from downstairs where the TV was when we were still a family. Then she'd play along with the practice cassette tape she kept in her dresser drawer year-round, serious as a heart attack to look at her face. All during *Gunsmoke*, you'd hear the big soft notes hanging in the air. It sounded funny then, her all alone like that.

I guess I hadn't thought on all that business about the pageant and home in quite a long while.

"Look at Ed McMahon," Matty said. He had the remote control in his hand. "He's like somebody's friggin dog."

I said, "It's three-thirty, it's going to take us a while to get there."

Outside, it might as well have been September. No snow at all. Matty squinted at the sun and said, "I'm glad I'm not from here. This is nothing."

We crossed the empty parking lot and ran across the highway and went through the tall weeds underneath the viaduct for the old tracks and then over the trainyard where box cars and tankers sat still on their steel wheels like they'd been there for forever. I saw that my brother needed some new shoes pretty bad—his black basketball sneakers were faded to white at the tip of each toe. I think I planned on stopping at a shoe store after we got Clarence's money, but it never happened. Things changed pretty fast. There was a lot of cash.

We passed over a high school football field with a rubber track running around it and then cut through a thin bit of woods before finding the sidewalk that ran into town. We saw the Western Union sign hanging off a supermarket gable at the far end of the deserted street and walked down the yellow line toward the electric doors. It was quiet everywhere. It must have been Christmas.

WESTERN PENNSYLVANIA

THE TAPPING on the wall started again. The sound came from right over the TV, which was on with the sound turned down, showing an old movie of men rowing the giant oars of a big open boat. The sky and the sea were the same bluest blue. Karen rubbed her cigarette out and noticed for the first time that the orange blob that was printed on the ashtray under the words *New Jersey* was supposed to be a tomato. Or an orange, if oranges ever had green stems. She thought back to Florida but couldn't remember.

The baby was sleeping on his back on the other bed, his tongue barely poking out of his mouth. Karen had piled up the pillows around his little body to keep him from rolling off onto the floor. His hand was clutching the corner of a pillowcase. The motel clerk tapped from the motel office in the next room and broke the silence again, a one-two-three made by rolling fingers on the other side of the thin wall. She heard a noise that might have been the muffled voice of the clerk but also might have been a semi downshifting out on the Interstate.

She looked back at the tomato or orange or whatever it was on the ash tray. It bothered her that she couldn't figure out which it was. Why couldn't they be more specific?

The ceiling was the suspended foam kind, and a broad brown stain fanned wide across a corner of the room except for one white rectangle where a panel had been replaced. It didn't seem like oranges could grow in New Jersey. She thought she'd been there once, a long time ago in a car when things were different. The New Jersey Turnpike? It didn't seem right that New Jersey could be famous for its tomatoes, either. Why was there a New Jersey ash tray here in the first place? Karen was pretty sure they were in Pennsylvania now. It had been late when she'd gotten off the Greyhound bus at the gas station depot and walked across the street toward the motel, pulling the wheeled suitcase behind her and balancing the baby's head against her neck. The air was too warm to feel like Christmas, but was cooler than Florida. *North*, she thought, *I'm still going north*. The thought of it made her smile, but also made her stomach play tricks.

The bus was gliding back onto the Interstate at the top of the on-ramp before she realized she'd left the bag with her pad of paper and pens and tarot kit behind. The realization gave her pain in her back. There was so much to remember all the time. So much to carry—diapers and shoes and then the dirty clothes in a plastic bag plus the radio and earphones and her cards on top of everything else. She had started to swear, but the baby was awake then and she didn't want him to get distressed. She knew she could fake a reading anyway. It wouldn't be the first time.

The clerk behind the counter at the motel had said, "Just the two of you?" and looked down at her hands. He gave her the key and said he'd be there always if she needed him. He smiled big teeth at her. She saw how his hair grew down over his ears like he was covering them up out of embarrassment. There was a painted ceramic frog in a Santa suit pinned to his shirt pocket. He gave her a key to the room adjacent to the motel office.

Sadness is part of life, she told herself again, it's a lesson we all learn. She was making things better.

Karen lifted her hips up off the bed and fit two fingers into her front pocket. There were a few pieces of folded paper in there, six twenty-dollar bills, a ten, two ones and the Medic-Alert medallion she'd found in the jewelry case of a Christian thrift store in Davenport, Iowa while running north from Florida half a year ago: to her sister's place outside Eau Claire. That was when the baby was brand new. She'd stayed there for a few weeks, but then found a way to let what she'd left in Florida call her back, just like always.

She stacked the bills on the bedspread and pressed the medallion to her forehead. The curve of the metal fit the contour of her brow and warmed her skin there. She pressed it to her lips and felt the lines of the engraved snake wrapped around a staff. Blue light from the television played dully across the ceiling. She raised the medallion up toward the stained panels and saw where it said *Allergy To Penicillin* in red letters and where she'd scratched the word *BABY* into the surface with the leather punch of a jackknife she'd borrowed from a man she'd let kiss her outside a bar during her stopover in Davenport last summer. The scratches had worn down a little from rubbing around in her pocket for the past few months. She told herself to remember to fix that.

Karen counted the money again and then counted the money again. One-hundred and thirty-two dollars. Enough to see them through a few days at the motel plus enough to get to the next place, north or south. A few days here, in between, might make up her mind. There was a thin phone book and a Bible on the nightstand. The phone book named a few towns on the cover, but didn't say which state they were in. She checked the white pages for Western Union and saw the eight-hundred number and two local listings—one on Lawrence Street and one on the Interstate, probably a truckstop. She could work the phone for a few solid days and get Andy to wire her the money. He'd hit her for a few dollars on top of the Western Union percentage, which would cut into her earnings but was better than going without. Karen told herself maybe there might be a Christmas goodwill to soften the situation but knew there'd be nothing.

A barechested man with a beard and a kind of skirt was standing up in the boat. His body was surrounded by pure blue. All the other half-naked men were looking up to him with adoration in their eyes as he argued with a man in a helmet and breastplate—a Roman, she thought, a bad man. The man with no shirt might have been Jesus, but Karen couldn't remember anything about Jesus being on a boat with any Romans.

She unfolded the pieces of paper until she found the

one with StarPhone Psychic Hotline's number. She had other numbers, but only Andy was reliable when it came to wiring cash. The ink was blurry from getting wet a long time ago.

The phone rang once and Andy's voice came on the line. He said, "Andy."

"It's Karen Power."

"Karen! Karen, I can barely hear what you're saying. You sound a million miles away like on Mars or something."

"My baby's sleeping."

"That's fine but you speak up when the clientele calls you? Open your mouth wide—*smile when you dial*, you know?" She could hear him stretch his mouth when he said the words.

"I know."

"And don't tell them Merry Christmas. We got Jews and shit calling *all* the time."

"I know."

"You're where?"

"At a hotel. You have your pen?"

She gave him the direct number for her room. "No calls after midnight, okay? You bother my baby."

"What time zone are you?"

"East. Like always."

"I'm east, too, you know. You might have to pay Andrew a real visit someday."

She tried to say something back but her mouth didn't make any sound. The phone clicked and then Andy's voice said, "I have to fly away, sweetheart."

She held the dead phone until a robot voice said "If you'd like to make a call, please hang up and try again."

The man in Davenport was named Dennis and he had a beard that split into two parts. He told her about how the local kids put tube socks over their arms to work the cornfields in the summer, loosening the tassels of the corn plants to make them breed right. He made a joke she didn't understand. He told a story about a busload of those kids getting stuck in high water during the floods a few summers back. Some boys got out to go for help and got washed away. One body turned up in Missouri. He told her a lot of things and bought her a cranberry juice with a slice of lime and a squirt of 7-Up in it. The baby was sleeping on a blanket on the floor. It was early and the only other people there were old men except for the bartender, who stayed way at the other end of the bar until Dennis would nod to him. They knew each other's names.

She allowed herself one glass of Blue Ribbon beer and then one more. Dennis said the Pabst brewery in Milwaukee was going out of business any day now. He had a friend on the inside.

She told him about the baby. How he was born too soon and sleeps all the time. Dennis nodded and didn't say anything.

Later, she let Dennis push his beard against her face where they stood in the tall grass behind the bar. The exhaust fan in the air conditioner rattled next to her ear and leaked a narrow stream of water over the siding where she kept her hand until he reached for it and held it against his groin while he kissed her on the neck. She pulled away and kept her shoulders up by her ears as she hurried back around the corner and into the bar where the baby was drooling a dark spot onto his blanket. She remembered the feeling in her spine that said his hands might reach out for her at any second, but the man named Dennis didn't follow her back inside and she was grateful for that.

The phone rang and the baby shook his head, worked his mouth, made an engine noise but didn't wake up.

WESTERN PENNSYLVANIA

A girl named Faye didn't say hello. Karen recognized her voice, the way she made a wet sound when she said her S's. Faye said, "Female calling from seven-one-eight New York, okay?" Faye was gone and there was silence while the bill added up. Karen heard a clicking and then a woman on the phone said she couldn't afford but a minute and was in a hurry anyway. She said "great rush." Karen thought she sounded German, though she couldn't remember ever meeting anyone from Germany. There was noise in the background like the German woman was calling from a payphone. There was the sound of a siren passing by and when it quieted again, the woman was saying, ". . . one card only please, one card quickly."

Karen knelt down by the baby's bed and smoothed out the blanket around his squat little body.

The woman on the phone sounded young. Karen imagined her standing on a corner a million miles from home, a StarPhone leaflet in her hand. She heard herself speak in the deeper, certain voice that only came out when she was working, "The Sun. The nineteen card." She pictured it in her mind, the two figures standing together under a smiling flat-faced sun like the kind hippies used to sew onto their bluejean jackets. She started to say, "Success if you trust and forgive yourself—" but the woman hung up before Karen had a chance to stretch out the cost. With all the street noise gone from the phone, the room seemed more silent than before.

She went to the window and looked out across the narrow parking lot and past the gas station to where the Interstate passed by. Cars flew in both directions. There were people in Massachusetts she could rely on for a time. They'd told her as much. There was Florida, too, and the misery she always intended to stay away from.

This place was nowhere. She could put her foot down in either direction and start over.

When she'd stood there in the tall grass with the man named Dennis, she imagined herself watching him and her. Lonely was all she was.

She heard the fingers tapping on the wall behind the TV. One-two-three, one-two-three, one-two-three. She could see the man behind the desk in her mind. The way he swallowed and looked at her hands when he said, "Just the two of you?"

Karen got up and walked over to the television, where the men from the boat were now on the shore, silently fighting a giant monster made from rock. Everybody does get lonesome. She leaned her elbows against the TV and ran the pads of her fingers over the wall. It had been painted with a sponge or a rag and looked red underneath the wash of yellow. She blew a string of hair out of her eyes and tapped on the wall with her fingers. One-two-three. She waited a few seconds and did it again. The television box was warm under her arms. She heard his fingers drum on the other side of the wall. A horn honked somewhere outside and then another one honked from somewhere farther away. Nothing here was permanent.

His fingers tapped again, further to the right. She put her ear to the yellow wall and followed the muffled taps as they moved along the wall, one-two-three, one-two-three, tapping along as she sidestepped with their movement, closer and closer to the door.

The baby opened his mouth and made a sticky complaint but didn't open his eyes. She whispered "Sleep baby," and took the key from the windowsill. The door opened and closed without making a sound.

THE THIRD ROOM

THIS FELLOW ED had reached the point where he had to sleep sitting up in the armchair because the colossal weight of his own body would crush his lungs in the night. With money from the state, he paid for the room and food, which he ordered on the phone from a restaurant in town that delivered. After all this time, that's about what I remember of him.

I slept on blankets in the bathtub and got a few boys for him in trade for lodging when I was about to turn twenty-two. It was an arrangement we had. He paid money to put his mouth on them.

I found them at the only bar nearby, Shangri-La's, which was really just three stools and a countertop with a pair of short refrigerators full of beer cans holding it up. They'd be trying to pass off as older than they were, wearing their church shoes and speaking in adult tones, trying not to laugh. The man behind the bar was not as smart as he pretended to be, with his dyed hair and liver spots on the backs of his hands, but he must have known they were under age. With no one else around to patronize his bar, they served to complete the picture in his mind.

I'd gotten involved in this situation myself when my predecessor, a skinny guy named Van, found me sitting at that same pitiable bar telling embellished stories and still convincing myself that it wasn't too late for me to go back to college without anyone noticing I'd been gone. Van said he was living with a fat homosexual, but that he'd had enough. The fat man, who's name was Ed, had cats that gave Van hayfever and made his ears itch like someone was rubbing cotton against tinfoil in the exact middle of his brain. Van said this to the ceiling as much as anybody.

"He's just *there* all the fucking time," he said. His name may have been Vaughn. It's hard for me to remember.

He gave me the room number and later, while the bartender was gone from his bar, I left. I knew just where the motel was because I had been living there myself ever since I'd first gotten off the highway a week earlier, adding up quite a sum on a Discover card I'd managed to secure when I first started school.

This was in the far end of Pennsylvania. Lines of cars roared both ways on the highway like trains on tracks. You could hear them all the time.

This Ed had a cream-colored toilet seat device with grips—loops of steel welded onto the sides like robot wings. It sat on top of a special box next to his unused bed and that's where he made his waste. I don't know anything more about it.

The bathroom was my own. I had the blankets and pillows in the tub and took out three of the light bulbs from over the mirror so it wasn't too bright when the switch was "On." I never saw any of the cats Van spoke of.

I didn't like being in Ed's room. I missed staying in Room 6 by myself with two beds and a bathroom with a heat lamp which made the skin on my back feel good while I brushed my teeth. But I had reached the end of my credit card and was down to the last of my paper birthday money. A simple decision that was barely a decision at all, made during a dark mood. A passing car and a thumb, and now, Ed, always in the armchair in the shadowy corner over by the television with his short arms tucked over the mass of his torso, his small hands clutching each other. Even from within the bathroom, I could

179

sense him out there in his chair, silently living. But for all his size, sometimes it seemed like I could walk over to him and put my fist through the place where he appeared to be darkly sitting.

If you laugh about it and make it sound like an uncertain lark, then the boys you might meet at the bar will laugh too. And then, as likely as not, and more likely than you might suspect, one will call the number you give him: those uncertain young men struggling around in bewildered yearnings. The phone would ring and Ed would prop himself over on one elbow to speak quietly and clearly into the receiver. Like that, with his big thick glasses on his head, he looked like the most confident human I've ever seen. I don't want to overstate things. I only got a few boys. The truth is, even fewer than that.

The bartender with the liver spots got sort of tired of seeing me at his bar, Shangri-La's, which really was just a corrugated vinyl shed practically like the kind you can find as a ready-to-assemble kit in a big hardware store outside of a town. It sat in his yard, in the shadow of his house. When I'd show up he would put two hands on the counter and then push a towel around for a minute. He'd give me a look so as to satisfy himself that he'd established an order of power. Then he'd padlock the refrigerators, cough, and walk out of the little room and into his house for a while. I knew that tending bar had been some kind of dull lifelong dream for him. The beer came from a grocery store in cardboard cases of twenty-four.

I played the lonely pinball game in the corner of Shangri-La's. The sound didn't work any more and one of the flippers didn't respond to the human touch. There was no music in the place, and the dead clickings of the game died in the still air. Allowing the tarnished ball to bounce from the sick flipper over to its healthy, powerful twin took all of my concentration, but the more I focused, the more I wasn't there, doing that. The door to the coin safe was left open, so you could retrieve your quarter and play as many times as you wanted.

This was the season when nobody knew where I was. It seemed as though I had stopped time and come off the highway into some other place while all that I'd left stayed waiting for me in the distance. It seemed as easy as just returning, then.

A particular boy started to call Ed every day.

If he came in the night, I could lean my face against the acrylic shell of the bathtub and in my mind follow the graceful arc of the pinball as it noiselessly swept across the painted table, glancing away from the lit targets and flying up to the top of the plane before losing speed and falling straight back to the dead flipper, from where it would bounce across the channel to the other and get catapulted back into space. Eventually I'd hear the room door click shut as the boy would leave. This wasn't how I had imagined life.

Just before Christmas, I was at Shangri-La's drinking from a twelve-ounce can of Budweiser beer. There was a smiling fellow a year or two older than me sitting there in a blue workshirt. The bartender was smiling when I walked in, but turned sour when he saw me, and soon left, which gave me a certain satisfaction. The fellow in the blue shirt seemed too old for Ed, and I was ready to give up all that business and find my way back to the college anyway. My shoes and pants and books and a three-hundred-dollar electric guitar and a new typewriter were all still in a dormitory room in a different part of the state where there were old buildings and girls with fault-less hair. It had been so easy to let my mind wander and put out a thumb on the edge of campus.

The smiling person sitting next to me said, "You live

in that room with the heavy guy and the cats, don't you?"
His accent was one I didn't know exactly.

I made no answer that I can remember, and he said, "I just stole my brothers' car. They don't even know it yet."

An hour slipped by like that, we two at the bar.

He wanted nothing from me and I rode in his Mercury with my face against the window, watching the pinball of my mind's eye glide over guard rails and the plain horizon, rising into the gray winter sky and easing back to Earth. He took me to Atlantic City, New Jersey, where I went down to the filthy water and prayed for home.

FOUR MILES OUT

WITH BAD WEATHER and no work for anybody, Dean had been waiting for a break in the snow and wind for the one job they *could* do. When he woke in the darkness before dawn to the sound of quiet, he peered through the curtains of his bedroom and made out the whirligig on the front porch turning a lazy circle. Downstairs, he found his thermos under the sink, put tea water on to boil and called the others from the phone in the kitchen.

The basement was filled with cardboard boxes of whirligigs his great uncle Lyle had made before his heart finally gave up. Most had forest scenes with deer or moose painted on the sides. Others had almost-naked women copied from *Playboy*. They'd likely stay down there in the basement until after Dean was just as dead and gone as Lyle.

He arrived at the boat landing first and stood waiting for the others between two boathouses. His little Chevrolet had slid into a ditch near his house in late December and was, after two months of snowplowing, barely visible. He'd walked on the frozen dirt of the access road up to the dam, where the lake becomes the river, and crossed over to the boat landing. He could have asked the others to pick him up at home, but didn't want to seem needy. But now, despite his sweatshirts and canvas coat, he found himself standing like a hunchback to avoid touching the cold of his clothes from the inside.

Years earlier, frostbite had seeped into Dean's toes as he drank vodka from a plastic jug and stood with others too long in a snowy clearing while a bonfire burned away a pile of branches. He'd been wearing leather basketball sneakers and woke to feel a deep pain in his feet. They got cold easily after that. As he waited for his brother, Everett, and the others—Gary and Simone, he wiggled his toes for warmth. Each foot was packed in two white socks and the plastic bag from a loaf of bread. Year after year, his feet carried a cold dampness from October through to April.

They were going to cut ice for the icehouse at the camp on the little island four miles out from the dam. It was a once-a-year job he'd inherited before winter set in. It would take until dark and he hoped his feet wouldn't turn on him.

Dean lit his first cigarette and was pulling his glove back over his fingers when he heard the faint sound of Everett's new snowmobile crossing the bridge down-river from the dam. Dean followed the sound as it got closer and was surprised to see Gary's pickup come over the rise, Everett following behind, wearing a facemask and his hood up over his head. The box sledge hitched to the snowmobile's trailer knob drifted sideways a little as he slowed to come down the grade.

Gary turned the truck in a wide arc that brought it alongside the spot where Dean was standing. The truck's heater core was still dead and nobody had made the trip to town for the thirty-dollar part, so Gary and Simone sat in the cold cab with their chins tucked down inside their collars. Their black retriever, Merveil, sat between the seats. Clouds came out of her mouth.

They turned their eyes toward the window and Dean said, "Take it slow." He sat up on the flatbed and swung his legs around. A spare tire was frozen to the planks and he leaned against it for support before nodding to Everett. His brother cocked his head and lifted his thumb in a way that meant, *You can ride with me.* Dean answered by nodding his head back toward the truck's rear window in a way that meant, *Less wind here.* Everett waved back, *Suit yourself,* with both hands and then spun the snowmobile around to hit the lake from where kids swim in the summer. The wooden float lay stuck in the ice forty feet from the beach. Somebody had forgotten to take it in after Labor Day. It had gotten tossed up by the ice and Dean could see the blue plastic fifty-five gallon barrels that made it buoyant in water. He wondered if they might be squeezed to worthlessness before ice-out.

Everett was on the lake and quickly out of sight, around the horn of the boathouse inlet. Gary put the truck into reverse and Dean's head lolled back against the rear window of the cab, the cuff of his wool hat cushioning the bounce. They went down the boat landing and out onto the ice.

Snow clung in irregular patches, windswept and thin. The way Lyle had told it, wind comes down from the top of the world, across Canada and the north and sweeps the lake clean of snow. The wind can come up suddenly, gathering speed as it blows downlake. Sometimes it takes trees with it as it goes. In the summer months, the sky will turn a copper color every so often and a wall of water will get shoved down the lake. You've got to watch for that, he said, telling a story about guiding in the widest part of Short Tail Lake. The sky turned amber and he ordered his sport to reel in. They'd been trolling the lake all day and the first tank of fuel conked out on them just as Lyle swept the square-ended canoe around to head for shore. He was running a long fuel line because of the wind, keeping the tank up front for weight, and knew they didn't have time to move everything around to get the second tank hitched up. He told the sport to drop his rod and start paddling. They paddled to beat the devil for half a mile and Lyle said when they reached shore he looked back and saw the wall of water ripping by, not even taking time to break over itself. Jimmycane is what he called it, but Dean had never heard anyone else use that word and wondered if Lyle had simply made it up. Then, if he let himself dwell on it, he wondered if Lyle had made up the whole story just so he could tell it.

As the dam grew smaller at the end of the lake, Dean looked off to the sides and saw the little village of bobhouses and pick-ups. It was barely dawn, but most of the chimney ducts had smoke coming out of them, rising straight up into the cold air. He saw Brian Bailey skimming the night's growth of ice out of the holes surrounding his shanty with a plastic milk jug cut down to make a scoop. They waved to each other. He looked to the other side of the truck and saw a man he couldn't recognize drilling new holes with a blue ice auger near the place where an Indian had once gone through the ice in his pickup. Dean tried to make out how deep he was drilling, but couldn't.

He and Everett had built a bobhouse one summer—twin benches, yellow fiberglass insulation behind lauan paneling, a window salvaged from the collapsed part of the house—but a low branch ripped the roof open as they trailered it to the landing. The disassembled pieces of it had leaned against the back of Everett's woodshed ever since, waiting to be rebuilt.

They passed the enormous boulder that lay half-submerged in ice at the shoreline. Dean had been watching for it. It marked halfway to the camp on the little island. Dean couldn't look at it without seeing the wrinkled face of an old man in the crisscrossing cracks. The trees on both sides of the lake spread off to the sides and the plane of ice grew twice as wide. A summer cabin peeked out from the trees on one side, plywood covering its two front windows. Ice-covered rocks from the county quarry lined the high, steep bank up to the camp to stop erosion. The white triangle of the bank looked soft in the distance, but Dean knew its surface was blown shiny and hard from the wind's rushing by in a hurry to squeeze into the bottleneck formed by the two shorelines.

He looked over his shoulder and saw Gary and Simone leaning against their doors. Simone had a glove off and was stroking her fingers over Merveil's ears. He noticed her wedding ring and was surprised she hadn't taken it off by now.

Gary and Simone had come from St. Stephen. They were New Brunswick French and spoke in a secret language when nobody else was close by. Gary had come across the border to work in the woods, cutting pulp for Georgia-Pacific on a temporary visa two winters back, when Everett was still working a log crane. Simone came to meet him that spring. She'd been working second shift for Flakeboard and hated living like that. When she first came over the border, Dean found himself shy when they were together. Everett seemed to notice but didn't tease him. She didn't speak often, and her accent hung heavily on her words. It often seemed that her thoughts were elsewhere, deaf to the young men nearby. When she receded into herself like that, her sleepy expression made Dean take notice of how dull and thoughtless their conversation had been and made him silently embarrassed. Gary told stories about people from St. Stephen and laughed about their old friends and Simone's husband like they weren't even real. The first October, Gary and Everett used Merveil for ducks in the Indian Town marsh. They all knew that INS needed nothing more than one speeding ticket to take notice and send them back across the line to what they'd left behind. They stayed close to the house trailer they cash-rented from a summer fisherman and avoided town as best they could. Dean knew there was no way it could last.

HE CRANED his head around again and saw the island through the windshield. He was surprised at how close they were already. The truck bounced a little on the snow that lay unblown in the lee of the island. Gary followed Everett's snowmobile tracks fifty yards offshore, slowly, the tire chains crunching on the snow. They came around the horn of the small cove to where Everett was sitting sidesaddle on his snowmobile. He was smoking a cigarette with his facemask pulled down below his chin.

The rear tires bumped over a lump in the ice and Dean fell back onto the flatbed. He pushed himself up onto his elbows but flopped back against the spare tire when Gary stopped the truck suddenly and opened up his door, leaned his head out and asked, "You have a place in mind?" Merveil squeezed out of the cab over Gary's lap and jumped to the frozen surface of the lake. She tried to run but her paws couldn't hold on the ice. She loped in place and then lost her balance, falling hard on her jaw. Simone clucked her tongue and said something in French that Dean couldn't hear. Gary turned to her and said something back, laughed at his own joke.

Dean scooted to the side of the flatbed and pushed himself over the edge so that he was standing next to Merveil. She bounced up on her hind legs and pawed at his stomach, barking happily. He thought about rubbing her ears but decided it was too much effort in the early morning cold. She blinked at him and swallowed, wagging her tail.

"We want to be out a little bit farther where the ice is thick, over beyond Everett a little ways."

It seemed reasonable to Dean that the ice would be thicker in the deeper part of the little cove, but knew it was hard to predict. Years ago, in the unspoken annual race to be the first out, the first to drill fishing holes and set flags, the Indian from the Indian Town had gone through the January ice in his pickup. They had to dredge for him in May. Just a week after the Indian went under, Dean heard that Robert DeFoe's father had gone out on the ice, inching forward towards the deep in his own pick-up with the door open, listening. What could he have done if he'd heard the boom of ice giving out? Speed? Run for his life? Dean remembered Lyle's words: *five inches of black ice will hold a horse*. He could see the great flatness of the upper lake stretched out in the distance as he walked to his brother. Merveil tried to follow. She bobbed her head as her paws skittered out from beneath her. Dean watched Gary ease the truck forward with a leg still hanging out the door and wondered, Who knows what a horse weighs?

Everett was taking tools out of the sledge and brushing away snow with his long mittens. He handed Dean the push-broom and grinned at him, a new cigarette bitten between his front teeth.

"You look a little chilly."

"I might just as soon be in bed."

"You remember the key?"

Dean patted his jacket's breast pocket with a gloved hand.

He stepped around his brother and began sweeping off snow. The ice looked cloudy underneath. *Ten inches of black ice will hold a team of horses.* He turned the broom at a right angle and cleared another strip, five paces long. Another turn, another five paces. He looked up as he cleared the final side and saw the other three standing by the snowmobile, admiring its red and yellow newness. He still hadn't asked what kind of debt Everett had taken on to buy it dead in the middle of winter. Everett had disconnected the old homemade sledge and pulled it back a few feet so the vision of the machine wouldn't be tainted. Gary stood resting a boot atop the Jonsered chainsaw that he'd stolen from the company when he quit cutting pulp. He leaned on the other, shorter saw like a walking cane at his side. Dean squared off the clear field he'd made with the broom. Then he went over the bare ice carefully, as Lyle had told him to do, brushing vigorously at the tenacious patches of crystallized snow until they turned to powder and he could push them away.

"Take me up to the icehouse and let's get it straightened out."

Everett nodded and started his snowmobile before stepping over the seat, revving the throttle with his thumb, lurching the snowmobile forward a few inches. Dean climbed on behind him and got one glove under the hand strap. They crossed the cove and bumped up onto the shore over ice-covered rocks. Everett followed a straight line through the trees to the icehouse. He cut the engine and Dean heard Merveil bark out in the cove.

Hemlock branches drooped onto the asphalt roof under the weight of snow, forming a dark canopy over the clearing around the icehouse. They dug out a space in front of the door, piling the snow to one side and uncovering green and brown moss spotted with clumps of dirty frost below.

Everett kicked at the bottom of the icehouse door to free it where it had frozen and then gestured at Dean for the key to unlock the big Yale padlock. Dean fished it from his pocket without removing his glove.

"Good thing they keep this locked," Everett said, pecking at the lock with the key, chipping ice. "Especially with the big shortage this season." He looked up at Dean.

Dean smiled back. "It's to keep the French out."

"Surprise," Everett said, "It's all frozen. You got your lighter handy?" Dean pulled off a glove with his teeth and brought his pack of cigarettes out from his breast pocket. He passed a bent cigarette to his brother before shaking the plastic lighter out of the pack. Everett took it and adjusted the flame so that it burned high and held it under the keyhole.

Out on the lake, a chainsaw started and died, started again. Dean heard the engine rev and then slow to an idle. Everett turned to him and said, "I can fix this up in here. You want to go make sure they don't start doing it wrong," and turned back to the lock. Dean looked out toward the truck and the ice field and tried to see Simone and Gary through the trees. He couldn't.

"Okay," he said and slid his arms into his jacket pockets. "You mind if I take the sled? I'll go easy."

Everett turned to him and lifted his eyebrows, "That's right you will." But he was smiling.

He followed their tracks back to the cove, packing down the trail.

Lyle had explained how to do the cutting. He'd told Dean to clear a field, five square paces with a little room on the outside to keep things comfortable. Cut a grid with a short saw so as to leave plenty of solid ice between you and the water at the cuts. Use the big saw and a crowbar when you're ready to start packing the blocks. You want to work slow. You want to keep your head on what you're doing. It's easy if you keep your head on what you're doing.

Gary and Dean would stay down on the lake, Gary cutting and Dean yanking the sawn blocks aside with ancient steel tongs. Lyle said the ice is heavy, but if you push a block down into the water, it'll leap back and you can boost it right up out of the lake. Simone would run the blocks up to the icehouse with the snowmobile. Everett would pack the blocks in snow and then in sawdust. They'd keep their heads on their own jobs.

Lyle had twisted his face up and told Dean that the Indian who went through the ice had been a fool. He'd come over the road that crosses the marsh between the Indian Town and the lake and went right out onto the ice from the boat landing above the dam. He made it to just short of the half-way rock before the ice coughed and split from both sides, leaving a jagged gash in the lake for thirty yards in both directions and a mess of water and broken ice at the hole. Dean thought that surely the Indian must have tried to open the door. His truck must have stayed partly out of the water for a few moments—long enough for the Indian to get out through the window at least. Or maybe not. Maybe the ice kept the door shut tight. Maybe he disappeared under the water before he could escape through the window. The water must have filled the cab just slowly enough to make dying awful. The state police boat dredged for him in the spring with large hooks and a deck-mounted crane. Lyle knew one of the troopers. He said the Indian's body was inside the cab when they pulled him up. His skin came apart in their hands. Foolish is the same as dead, according to Lyle. Only a matter of time.

Dean killed the snowmobile's engine and nodded to Gary in a way that said, *You about ready to do some damage with that saw?*

Gary nodded his head, the small chainsaw idling in his hands. "How many cuts?"

"Ten to one side, ten to the other. Try and keep them straight if you can. Not too, too big—foot and a half. Icebox-size." Lyle had picked him to take over the winter maintenance work out on the island. This was his job. A four-man job at least. The owners had his telephone number and would mail him the check when it was done.

The short saw's motor whined sharply, cutting off all

the natural sounds of the big frozen lake. Dean looked uplake and could see only the low, whitened hump of a low mountain that marked the far end of the water. It seemed almost impossibly distant. Everything under the flat sky beyond the cove was the white and gray of freezing cold.

Gary leaned over and held the saw away from himself to avoid the exhaust spray of slush as he waddled backwards, cutting lines. He was squinting in concentration, trying to keep the saw angled to cut deep but not all the way through. A thin pool of water gathered at the kerf. It froze quickly as the saw passed by and left a raised pearly stripe like scar tissue. Merveil stared at the noise and then ran to Gary's boots to nip at them playfully. He gently kicked her away.

Dean stood there in the freezing air and watched Gary shuffle backwards carefully, awkwardly, on one knee, now cutting the rows of perpendicular lines in the ice. Dean's feet were almost numb. He was glad they didn't feel wet. Too cold, even inside the plastic bread bags, for his feet to sweat. Cooling sweat was misery. He looked back to see Simone packing the dry snow from the truck's hood into powdery snowballs and gently lobbing them over Merveil, who barked quietly under the noise of the chainsaw and bounced up on her weak back legs to snap at the loose snow. Dean winced as Merveil's legs splayed out and her jaw hit the ice. He thought that she winced too, blinking her eyes a few times and licking her tongue out over her floppy black lips. Simone's face gave a gentle smile and she didn't look cold at all. He wondered how long she'd stay before going back. Was it possible she'd stay? Could she like it here better than anywhere else?

Dean looked up when he noticed motion at the shore and saw his brother stepping out onto the lake. His legs were white from the knees down where snow stuck to his wool pants. He raised his eyes for a moment while stepping carefully over the rocks onto the ice and threw up one arm in a wave as he looked back to his feet. Gary finished another cut and the motor rumbled rhythmically at idle as he waddled forward on his knees to make the next one, sliding the saw ahead of himself.

By the time Everett reached the truck, Gary had begun the last perpendicular cut. Simone had left off throwing snowballs for Merveil and sat in the truck with the door open and a leg dangling out, waiting for the cigarette lighter to pop up. Dean lit a cigarette of his own and didn't offer his lighter to Simone. The gesture seemed too intimate with Everett standing right there and, anyway, the chainsaw was too loud. The truck's lighter would be ready soon enough. Merveil lay on the ice with her head on her paws, watching, blinking. Everett leaned over as if to say something, but didn't.

DEAN AND EVERETT were sitting on the flatbed, looking uplake at the two big islands in the distance; they were hard to distinguish from the shore in the whiteness of it all. Dean was kicking his feet back and forth, caught up in the rhythm of it, bouncing his boot heels against the tire to keep his blood going. They'd been sitting there daydreaming in the resonance of the saw's buzz. It was the sound of the saw, the sudden acceleration as the chain found no resistance, that let them know something had happened. It was the break in the monotonous drone that made them turn, unhurriedly, to see Gary missing, gone under the lake. And it wasn't until they were around the truck, Everett slipping as he made the turn, falling hard on his elbow, that Dean saw that the grid of ice, detached and broken into sections, was teetering in the water. Simone and Dean got to the edge at the same time and dropped to their knees at the side of the hole.

Blocks of ice bobbed gently from side to side and then Gary's head and one arm seemed to float up from below, his hat gone and dark hair pasted over his eyes. Simone said something, reached out for Gary's arm and missed several times before seizing his coat sleeve. She pulled, but that only wedged Gary's head and shoulder between two blocks of ice, trapping him there. Dean took hold of Simone's coat and tried to hold her back from falling forward.

The ice shifted, pinching Gary and then releasing him back out of Simon's grip. He slipped down below the surface and was gone again. Water splashed up between blocks of ice. It took Dean a few moments to realize that Simone was telling him to move the ice. It took him a few more moments to think straight, to release his hold on Simone's coat and claw at the big slippery shapes of ice bobbing in the dark water. He knew even before he tried that he'd never be able to take hold of one.

Everett reached them. He had his elbow tucked against his ribcage. A shovel was in his other hand and Dean took it from him.

He tried to push at the nearest block—a solitary piece

which had come loose of the grid. The ice was shiny from turning in the water. It was white below the surface and made a beautiful shape inside itself like a paperweight Dean had seen, the fluff from a dandelion somehow captured in glass. The shovel's blade scraped across the top without taking hold. He heard himself grunt as he raised the shovel and tried to pull the ice closer. Simone was repeating something in French, staring at the place where, moments before, Gary's head had been, blinking and choking on lake water. Dean felt himself shaking and breathing too sharply through the nose. He leaned out with the shovel raised over his head and brought it down hard against the wet block of ice. It made a weak metallic sound. He hit it again, harder and nicked the glassy exterior. A white streak like lightning shot into the ice from the nicked surface. Everett was holding Dean's shoulder. He was shouting, trying to make him stop.

"Not these, not these," He was saying. Dean stopped, finally hearing his brother's voice.

"Those, those," He was saying, pointing at a loose row of blocks.

The ice seemed barely to move, but Gary's arms and then head emerged from a widening rift. His face looked like the face of someone having a nightmare. He was turning his head back and forth slowly, shakily, as if gesturing, *no, no, no* and mouthing something with his lip hanging open. Merveil danced from one side to the other, excited and barking at the hole in the ice. Dean held the shovel in one hand, the handle braced against his arm and leaned out as far as he could, shoving a block of ice away from Gary's ear with the blade. Simone lunged out across a row of floating blocks and seized Gary's forearm in both hands. Everett jumped to stand over her and pulled back on her coattail with one arm. As she slid back between Everett's legs, Gary came bumping up out of the water like an otter onto a bank. His mouth was bleeding and when Dean looked away and then looked again, he thought that Gary's front teeth might be broken.

Gary shifted on his side and coughed violently but then stopped, looked up at Simone, and smiled as she pulled his head up onto her thighs, smoothing his wet hair back over his head. It was already frozen into stiff spears. Everybody breathed out and smiled too. Dean felt his hand reach for cigarettes. But then Gary stopped smiling and didn't make much of a face at all.

Dean looked to Everett who looked to Simone, who had lowered her face to Gary's. Her back rose and fell with heavy breathing. Merveil hopped up and down on her hind legs, rubbing her face against Simone's arm. "Okay okay," Simone was saying. "Okay okay okay okay."

Everett got to his feet and looked down at Gary, lying there on the ice completely still. "We have to get him someplace warmed up right now." He stood bent over his own arm, keeping the elbow tucked against his side. His face was hard.

"Put him in the truck," Dean said, standing. "We'll get him to town. Somebody ought to see him." He looked up at Everett. "Right?"

"You mean the hospital?" Everett said.

Simone said, "That'll take so long." She looked confused, gazing up at Everett with her mouth open. Dean thought he'd never seen her look like that before.

When Dean and Simone held each other's arms under Gary's back and thighs and lifted him into the sledge, they had to drop him the last few inches but he didn't register any expression. He just slumped his head over onto his shoulder. Simone immediately started running stiff-legged toward the island shore with her arms straight down at her sides. Merveil bounded after her. Dean watched them for a second before climbing on behind his brother. He looked back and couldn't be sure if Gary was breathing. He decided not to look too closely. Gary's hair was white in spots. Everett pressed the starter and eased in on the throttle.

The icehouse was black inside. Everett had shoveled most of the sawdust up against the blueboard insulation in preparation for packing. A half-dozen blocks of ice from last winter's cutting were strewn around the doorway, shrunken slightly from a year's aging. Bits of sawdust clung to them. Dean and Simone lowered Gary to the floor. Merveil pushed between their legs and sniffed at the cedar sawdust. She lay down and rolled in it. Everett came to the door and his body blocked the light.

"God, move," Simone whispered at him. She pushed Merveil across the floor to the threshold, where she whined and skipped out between Everett's feet into the snow.

Everett said, "I've got coffee here," and passed Dean a green metal thermos before stepping to the side of the door, holding his broken elbow in his hand. Dean propped Gary's head up and tried to pour a little of the hot coffee from the thermos cap into his mouth. It ran out from the corners of his lips, which were oddly puffy and pale. Simone was fumbling at the buttons on Gary's shirt. Everett said, "If you're set, I'd better get going."

Dean put the thermos down in the sawdust and gave it a turn so it would stay put, gently lowered Gary's head, stood and went outside. His eyes took a few moments to adjust to the light. He motioned with his head for Everett to come around to the side of the icehouse.

"How long til somebody gets out here?" he said as softly as he could.

"It could be a while." Everett didn't turn, but unhitched the sledge from his snowmobile and then lifted the trailer tongue away from the hitch with one foot before kicking it aside.

"How long?"

"I can make your house in half an hour, forty minutes. Get on the phone. But it could be a while."

"Who do you call?"

"I don't know. I'll figure it out. There's a hospital helicopter in Bangor."

Dean rubbed anxiously at the hat on his head. "A helicopter?"

Everett's cheek muscles tightened. "He's fucking cold. You can't get that cold." He stepped over the seat and then stopped. "Who told you to make cross-cuts before you're ready to yank the ice? That's not how you do it." Dean opened his mouth to speak but his brother was gone, straight down to the lake. He watched his brother until the trees cut off his sight and he heard the noise of the engine rise in pitch as Everett leaned on the throttle. It would be trouble to turn the handlebars in any real snow with just one arm.

Simone had put her own coat over Gary and was packing sawdust all around him as though she knew exactly what to do. Dean could barely see her inside the darkness of the icehouse. He wondered if Everett would stop at the bobhouses to call ahead to the store from somebody's radio, have them try to call the EMTs. He wondered if Brian Bailey had a CB in his truck.

Dean looked to the tree tops and saw the strong hemlock branches bending under heavy white snow. He turned back to the door and stepped inside. Merveil followed him, quietly. Simone had her gloves off and was rubbing at Gary's face—his cheeks, his forehead, his chin, his nose. She breathed against Gary's skin and rubbed her hands there quickly and gently. She was whispering something unknowable. It sounded like singing.

Simone looked up, her hands still rubbing Gary's face. "Shut that door."

"I'm going to take the truck and try to beat Everett to a radio. They must have one at that camp downlake."

Simone's face was turned back to Gary's. "Please shut that door."

Dean stood and stepped outside. "The one downlake. Where it gets skinny. Halfway." He looked back at Simone but Simone seemed to have forgotten him. "I might have to break a window. I'd better take the crowbar." In the darkness of a corner, Merveil was invisible to him. "Maybe you want to lie down by him. For heat."

He stepped out of the icehouse and onto the packed snow where the snowmobile's tracks led down to the ice. The trackbelt had left a mark like a washboard in the snow. He took a few steps and then went back to the icehouse and closed the door without looking in. Then he followed the path between tree trunks down the slope to the lake. His feet were itching with cold and he stopped to shake each foot. They continued to itch.

The hole seemed ridiculously small. A skim of ice had already started to form up in the water between blocks, which lay there irregularly, rounded corners askew in the black water. Gary's chainsaw and gas can and dirty jug of bar lube looked out of place next to the hole. The shovel was there. The push broom was leaning against the truck's fender. The ice had been too thin for the short saw. Lyle had said five inches of black ice will hold a horse. This was bad ice—white ice, weak with snow between layers. *A horse?*

Dean went to the truck and got in. A muted buzzer sounded until he shut the door. It was quiet inside. He took the wheel in his hands and looked at its center, at the cloudy blue Ford oval and the little embossed bugles. It had been a while since he'd last sat behind a steering wheel. Months. He looked out across the lake at the whiteness everywhere. He couldn't make out the shoreline through the windshield and understood that the weather had changed. He looked to the rearview mirror and tried to see downlake toward the boarded-up summer cabin high up on its steep icy bank. There was nothing but white on the horizon. He wished Lyle were still alive.

SIMONE KNELT in the darkness of the icehouse with her bare palms laid flat on Gary's cold cheeks. Life had taken her this far, to St. Stephen and to Gary and across the border to this shack on an island. Life would take her to whatever came next, but in her mind, she was back in Saint-Quentin, remembering a song from her youngest days at school. Had someone been there to hear her sing sweetly in another language, he would have heard the words that meant

> "Spring is near," the rough hush of the wind.
> "Spring is near," the returning birds sing.
> "Spring is near," the busy birds whisper,
> "Mourn the loss of the last falling snow."
>
> Branches bud, the thicket awakens.
> Branches bud, the bees suck the vine.
> "Branches bud," the bees hum quietly,
> "Summer blooms will wither in the fall."

Outside, the breeze picked up and, for a minute, the hemlock branches came to life.

KNOWLEDGE

CARLTON SAT on the hot rubber membrane roof of the boathouse. The sun was on its way down, but the air hung heavy with August, felt like weight on his face and shoulders. The longer he waited on the roof, the better his chances of making it through the day without seeing anybody in town.

The crash of water from the dam sounded new, loud, something he couldn't have noticed without leaving for a while. They had three gates open, still trying to get the lake level down to normal after a long and wet winter.

Some little kids were playing in the shallow water of the boatlanding between the boathouses and the dam. A few mothers sat in folding chairs on the gravel beach, drinking out of big plastic mugs with built-in straws. Carlton had parked his father's truck on the rise above them and walked across the landing to the row of linked boathouses, all but one of which needed painting. Tammy Spaulding was there, with kids. Maybe hers, he wasn't sure. He hadn't seen her in quite a while. One of the boys looked a little touched.

She hadn't been at the service. But the way she pretended she didn't see him walking by, even when the boy moaned at him and clapped his hands, told Carlton that she was embarrassed. She'd been Brent's girlfriend back in school, for a while anyway, and now Brent had hanged himself from a tree at the end of July, soon after his twenty-third birthday. He'd done it on the island four miles out—at the summer place where he'd worked maintenance since Dean Small moved away, taking in the docks and poisoning the mice that ate up the old corn-cob insulation, cutting ice for the icehouse in the winter. The camp belonged to summer people from New York State who'd left for the season in June because even on the island the mosquitoes were still too bad and the weather too hot to be like the vacation they'd wanted. Carlton had come back for the service, to read the eulogy. To *mark the passage*, as the minister had said on the phone. He was a new minister. Somebody who had come to the Congregational Church in the time since Carlton had left town. The minister hadn't known either of them; not until one died and the other came home.

Carlton got the phone call early on a Saturday. The minister said, "I don't know what to tell you but to tell you that Brent Stewart died two days ago."

"What for?" Carlton answered, and knew, even in the fog of sleep, that his question didn't make any sense. He got out of bed and tried to feel the way he was supposed to feel, rubbed his eyes and splashed water onto his face trying to experience the reality of it. He called the human resources director at the laboratory and explained that he'd have to be gone for a week. She was very sympathetic and in his half-sleep he tried to make himself feel the grief she supposed he felt.

That was only a few days before.

Carlton could hear the kids splashing and squealing in the shallow water. He'd swum there as a kid himself. He crab-walked a little further down the pitched roof to make use of the growing shadow cast by the trees across the inlet.

When the sun went down and everyone in town was at home, sitting in front of electric fans watching television, he gathered his clothes and climbed down the side of the boathouse and in through the boat opening to where two square-end canoes were rocking in the water, gunwales bumping together in the dark, splashing slightly. He put on his pants and boots and felt his way along the wall to the door. A loon made a long two-note call from out on the lake as he climbed the short hill to the truck. It was still as hot as daytime.

Carlton's father was asleep on the couch with the light on and his glasses splayed out across is face, hanging by one ear. His bare feet stuck out from the loose-knit Afghan blanket somebody had made and were nearly translucent, the toenails thick and yellowy from a life inside Red Wing boots. Carlton pulled the light cord and put the room into darkness before following the hallway to the room where he'd slept growing up. He lay on his back and tried to imagine tying a rope around his neck and tossing the free end over a tree limb, a lamp-post, the rafter-tie of a hunting camp. It made his throat tickle and he touched his Adam's apple trying to make the feeling go away.

He stayed there until the rest of the night was over, remembering the lines of the eulogy he had spoken that morning and listening to the quiet faraway hiss of the water coming through the dam.

When it became light enough to see the plaster cracks

in his bedroom ceiling, Carlton heard his father cough, working phlegm from his throat. The screen door squeaked on its hinges and clicked shut as his father spat. The truck's engine turned over. A French-language station came loud over the radio and then got quiet when his father shut the door. Carlton leaned out of bed and found his watch in the pocket of his pants where they lay folded on the floor. Five o'clock. Earlier than it had to be for his father to start his drive across the marsh road to the Indian Town and then off into the woods on the other side—the same drive he had made forever. Carlton imagined him driving slowly today, taking his time, smoking an extra cigarette. He was grateful for his father's shyness. It made things that much easier.

He pulled his pants on and went out to the porch to smoke a cigarette himself. Dew hung in the patches of grass like cobwebs and old leaves lay flat on the blacktop. Carlton had first left home for the University in Orono, where he'd gone after his junior year of high school as part of the state program for Gifted and Talented Children. The offer came, and there was no saying no. He went to live in a yellow-painted room with one window that looked out over a stretch of grass to windows in another building looking back. The geology lab was empty on Saturday mornings except for the graduate student attendants who didn't look up from their own work very often. He made up stories about new friends and described the models of cars on the dealership lots in letters he sent home to Brent. It snowed less there than it did at home. The food at the college dining hall tasted good and you could eat as much of it as you wanted. Brent didn't write back, but there were school vacations when they'd drink beer in the woods with Franky Swan and Tammy Spaulding and the Small brothers. But Carlton knew he'd turned his back on something by leaving town. It seemed like a long time ago now.

He kept writing letters even after Brent and some of the other boys from home joined up with the Army and the Marine Corps after graduation and wound up sitting offshore in the Persian Gulf for most of a year. Carlton got a letter in his mailbox then. He carefully tore off the perforated edges and unfolded the thin blue aerogramme paper to read Brent's left-handed writing, leaning heavily to the right in capital letters.

THERE IS NOTHING TO DO EXCEPT FOR LIFT-
ING WEIGHTS AND WRITING LETTERS. SOME

GO ON SHORE BUT MOSTLY WE JUST SIT
HERE WAITING. SOME NEWS PEOPLE CAME
AND ASKED SOME OF US TO SAY HELLO TO
OUR FAMILIES. TAMMY SAID SHE SAW IT ON
TV FOUR OR FIVE TIMES. I THINK IT WASN'T
ON EVERYWHERE. MAYBE JUST AT HOME BUT
MAYBE YOU SAW IT TOO. ONE THING THAT
DID HAPPEN WAS THERE IS ONE MARINE WHO
GOT SOME LINE AND CAUGHT A WEIRD HUGE
FISH OFF OF THE SHIP. HE WANTED TO COOK
IT BUT NOBODY KNEW IF IT WAS SAFE TO EAT
OR NOT. HE THREW IT BACK. IT WAS QUITE A
FISH! WE ALL WISH WE COULD GO ON SHORE
AND GET GOING THOUGH I WISH YOU COULD
SEE HOW BIG THE SHIP IS!

He read to the end and flipped it over but nothing was written on the back. He taped it up over his desk in the little yellow room and stared at it absentmindedly when his attention drifted from his reading. The more he looked at it, the more it seemed like something Brent had written many times over. After a week or so, he took it down and put it in the desk drawer. At the end of the semester, he put it in the trash with the rest of his papers.

Carlton had stopped sending letters by the time he finished at Orono and went over to New Hampshire to live in an apartment and work for the Army Corps of Engineers at their sprawling Cold Regions Research and Engineering Laboratory. They had him testing the mechanical behavior of ice for purposes he wasn't fully entitled to know. He kept writing, occasionally, but those were really letters to nobody, to himself. He tucked them into books and they never got sent. Brent never wrote again.

In June, a letter came from his aunt. Carlton read that Brent had returned home from the Marines and was looking good, she'd seen him at the store. At the time, it struck Carlton as funny that his aunt had thought to make special mention of it.

It took him two days to get as far as the bus station in Bangor, and the minister picked him up there. Carlton had expected words of philosophical consolation, but mostly they rode in silence. They drove to a Ford dealership where Carlton sat in a chair as a salesman sold the minister a half-ton pickup in trade for his older one of identical model and color. The air-conditioning system pushed chilled air around the showroom and a persistent squeak came from a hidden duct. Carlton found levers attached to his chair that raised and lowered the seat. He tilted back, swiveled around. The minister and the salesman discussed financing and went over papers. Out on the lot, a boy with a wispy mustache peeled away the paper that listed the new truck's features from the driver's-side window, using a razor to scrape away the adhesive. When the boy finished with the new truck, he got into the old one and drove it somewhere out of sight.

They rode silently north past Lincoln, the stench of the papermill jabbing at Carlton's empty stomach. He watched the trees go by as they left the pavement to short-cut on the sandy dirt roads between stretches of blacktop. Some had been tagged with pink or blue or orange ribbons as a code to the paper company that had cut the wide roads through the softwoods, deeper and deeper into the forest where his father and everybody else worked—his father no longer running a saw or driving a skidder, but operating a Caterpillar feller-buncher that could drop and limb a tall tree in just a few seconds without anybody else helping. The Company had sent him out to Peoria, Illinois for classes when they made the switch to mechanized felling. He spoke often of the trip.

The Ford's new upholstery was clean. Carlton tried to take up as little space as he could, keeping his elbow off the armrest. His pants looked worn out against the unblemished gray fabric of the seat. He wished they could still be in the old truck.

When they reached Topsfield, the minister stopped at the gas station for potatoes in foil and hot dogs from the rolling rack. It was late and there were diesels loaded with logs idling in the dirt lot behind the building. Carlton could hear them from inside.

The minister put his elbows up on the table and rested his chin on his thumbs. He was trying to look at peace, but his knees bounced up and down beneath the table. "Are you nervous about speaking tomorrow?"

"I'm not nervous. But I feel a little funny about it."

"Funny how?"

"Like maybe there's somebody better for it."

"Your name came right up. Everyone told me that you were really close."

"We used to be more than now."

The minister looked down at some place between the two of them for a minute.

"At times like these, at certain times, people . . ." He

brought his hands down and pushed his fork back and forth across his plate, watching mashed potatoes rise up through the tines. "People expect someone to talk."

"I know. I've been to funerals. My mother's dead."

The minister didn't seem to hear. "Someone has to do it. I asked and people said you were the right choice. Was I wrong to ask you?"

"No. I would have asked me, too." The minister pursed his lips sympathetically, but Carlton knew he was relieved to be forgiven. He was from somewhere else.

He offered to listen if Carlton wanted to clear his mind before getting back to town. He offered to listen in case Carlton wanted to practice the eulogy a time or two. Carlton said no, and the minister just nodded. Later, when they pulled into Carlton's father's driveway, he said, "Look. Just say whatever you think sounds right. You can worry about the rest later."

Carlton looked out the window at the dark house. "Okay."

The minister put out his hand to shake and said, "Anyway, it's a eulogy, not an elegy, so remember that." He was grinning so Carlton knew it meant something comforting.

The next morning, Carlton sat with his father and his aunt in the center of the stone church. He sat leaning against the swinging door to the pew, hiding his head in his hand. Debbie Cummins played the organ. She had been Carlton's fourth and fifth grade teacher and looked just as she had then with her glasses on a beaded chain. Trees blocked the sun from the transept windows and the pulpit was lit by a green-shaded brass lamp, glowing weakly there in the half-light, not doing much good. The old people, women mostly, sat in the front rows, tilting their heads together to talk. Carlton knew them all. Their husbands had died of heart attacks or diabetes.

The minister introduced Wesley Maclean and Wesley walked to the pulpit. He'd joined the Marines with Brent while Carlton was away in Orono. If you join together, you serve together. The Buddy System. The recruiters came to the high school every year. Brent and Wesley had joined with Franky Swan, who was still in the Marines, making a life of it. On the day of Brent's service, he was said to be guarding huge tanks of drinking water in Somalia, but had sent a letter for Wesley to read at the occasion. To Carlton's ears, it was full of military extra-politeness. "Brent Stewart was the finest buddy a young man could have. Signed, Franklin Swan Junior, u s Marine Corps." Carlton remembered Franky Swan breaking the legs of a brown frog and slicing a small perfect wound into its throat with a black-handled Buck knife. They were fishing, twelve years old, in the marshy shallows of the river above the state fish hatchery with Brent and Dean Small. Franky put the frog back in the water and they watched it sink to the rocky bottom, where it drowned after a little while. Carlton made himself laugh but wished he could undo it when he saw that Brent was trying not to cry. Dean called Franky a prick and Franky waded out of the river to sit on a rock and chew some of the Levi Garrett he'd borrowed from his father's pouch. It occurred to Carlton, as he sat in the small stone church of his home, that he maybe had always sort of hated Franky Swan, who'd spent winter in Somalia and sent his words across the ocean to make an appearance in front of the whole town, to remind everyone of himself, to be a sort of hero. Carlton recognized his disdain as jealousy.

As Wesley Maclean stepped down from the pulpit and returned to his seat, Carlton fingered the eulogy in his jacket pocket. He'd written most of it on the first bus, from White River Junction to Boston. Then he rewrote it a half-dozen times between Boston and Portland, Portland and Bangor. He crossed out words and wrote different ones instead. He wrote the words in big letters so he could see them without straining, thinking the service could change things and he might have to read with wet eyes.

No glasses. He understood the vanity in that decision.

When the time came, he found himself at the front of the church, adjusting the gooseneck microphone. The minister had left a handwritten note to himself taped to the pulpit and Carlton felt like he'd learned a secret as he ran his finger over the words.

Lamentations 3: 31–33

Be honest.

B-R-E-A-T-H-E

The church door was propped open to let air in. He could see out over the road to the softball field and to the woods beyond. Brent's father was right in front, his eyes looking up. Carlton tried not to see, but when he noticed Brent's mother sitting there too, he was startled by how skinny she was now and in looking away caught Brent's father's eyes again. He looked down at his pages, leaned closer to the microphone and began speaking. He heard his voice coming from somewhere else and it sounded even and good, so after a few lines he looked up and saw faces looking back at him. A car slowly crossed the square of light at the back of the church.

It was over soon. He pushed the papers together and nodded out at the congregation. They kept looking at him, so he leaned back to the microphone. "He knew his life had run its course. It was just a shorter life than most of us get to lead."

Someone reached out for him and whispered *good job*. He touched the hand and kept moving. The minister was already talking again, reading from Romans, but Carlton saw people looking at him. Some didn't look at him, and he knew that meant something too.

After the minister had given as hopeful a benediction as he could, everybody rose and filed out by pew. It was then that Margaret Bonneau, who often spoke of Jesus, pushed her way to Carlton, eyes painted and wide. He found himself leaning back against his aunt and then Margaret Bonneau was shaking his hand in both of hers, saying, "That was wonderful what you said up there, you are a wonderful young man."

Carlton tried to speak words, but didn't come up with any. Then he said, "Thank you."

CARLTON RUBBED his cigarette out on the porch rail, leaving a stripe of soot on the red paint. He erased it with his hand. He looked up the road and saw Everett Small's little car come creeping around the bend. Everett threw an arm up in a wave, but then seemed to remember why Carlton was home, sitting on the porch, and changed his expression from a smile to a solemn look of hard sympathy as he passed by. Carlton followed the sound of the car as it bumped over the expansion joints of the bridge and made the turn onto the dirt road that ran upstream past the dam and though the woods along the lake.

He rose and breathed all the air out of his body before going inside and putting on his boots. On his way back out the door, he saw the note he'd missed earlier.

> *Carl,*
> *There is some food but not too much in the refrigerator and you can make the coffee or drink the beer later. There IS some coffee and beer too.*
> *from your dad*

Next to it was a twenty-dollar bill. He folded the note in half and put it in his pocket, leaving the twenty dollars anchored to the counter by a deck of worn playing cards held together by a rubber band.

Outside, somebody's kitten was jumping for grass-hoppers in the tall grass. He called to it on the way to the shed but it didn't care. Under the shed where the square-end canoe rested up on horses, Carlton found the paddle that his father had cut for him before he'd left for Orono. It only reached to his throat now. He leaned it back against the wall and went inside, his face catching thick, ropy spiderwebs just within the door.

Paddles lay in racks hanging from the ceiling—the racks that had once been used for lumber, back when he was still at home and they ran their own Woodmizer bandsaw out in the yard. Now that his father was alone, strips of masking tape with paddle lengths written in marker ink covered over where there had been, before, lumber dimensions scratched into the wood. Carlton's father made paddles at night. People liked them because they were good paddles. He shaped them with a sanding belt and sold them on consignment at the store in town and sent them through the mail if people called him.

They were teardrop shaped, not the rectangular or coffin shaped styles that had become popular. He could make good axe handles too, and people would bring their axe heads to him to get a new handle hung. In the corner, Carlton found a paddle that reached up to his brow. He liked them long to match his arms. He bent it against the floor to test its spring and flipped it over in his hands a few times to check the grip against his palm. In the center of the paddle blade was the burnt-in snowflake brand that his father used as a trademark. It was an uneven brand. The iron had darkened the space between the lines to a light brown. It had been in the corner as a reject, amongst others with warps or blanks with knots.

He remembered his father sweating in front of the burning woodstove in summertime with a barrel full of new paddles, heating the branding iron and pressing it to the wood, making a thin cloud rise to the ceiling. He'd put the iron back into the embers and blow on the brand before fingering it to make sure it was fine. Over and over again until they were all marked.

Carlton switched off the light and left the shed.

The kitten followed him across the yard and down the road a little while, diving for his bootlaces. And then it lost interest and trotted across the road to pick its way into the trees at the top of the bank. He swung the paddle through the long grass at the side of the road and listened to the swish of grass against the blade. It felt like a long time since he'd last walked down the road.

He'd packed his clothes and spent his last night in the little apartment back in New Hampshire. In the morning, he put his sheets and blanket in the suitcase and left his key on the kitchen counter. A taxi carried him first to the public library where he dropped a few books through the slot and then to the station in White River. Cars passed the bus and he watched the people inside as he struggled to write words about Brent, who was dead, and so hard to remember. Now he was home with no plans to stay, no plans to go. It didn't seem possible he could have forgotten so much in so little time.

He walked quickly with the paddle on his shoulder, hoping to get to the dirt road before running into anybody. But he slowed for a moment at the middle of the bridge and looked down at the water coursing beneath him. The river grew deep and narrow here, a quarter mile below the dam, and the water was even faster than usual with three gates open. He remembered getting in on the shallow side below the dam and wading out to where the current was strong. He and the others would swim deep below the surface as the bridge and the narrows came closer, somersaulting and swooping up or down with the entire weight of the river behind them, pushing. It was just like flying, Carlton thought, just like it.

They'd come up for air downstream from the bridge and struggle for the shallows just above the hatchery where Franky had drowned the frog. Below the hatchery, the river spread wide and turned white with fast water over rocks before calming again. And even then, only calm for a short stretch. They'd climb out at the hatchery and cross back over the bridge and walk up the paved road to the dam to wade into the fast water again.

Standing there over the river, Carlton saw the memory in his mind as a picture of the sky as it looked from under the water, the dark stripe of the bridge passing by above. He saw the pale flesh of Brent's body hovering in the periphery, faceless, but could remember no one particular time.

He left the pavement to walk on the access road in the cool shade of the woods. Through the trees, he could make out two men standing in the river, casting flyrods. At this time of year, they would have to be from far away, trying more to get away from something than to catch trout.

As he came out of the trees at the head of the access, the sound of the dam became deafening and he saw a group of men on the boardwalk over the gates. They were all pushing up on one of the long wooden levers, closing the third gate down to half, looking like the picture of Marines at Iwo Jima, except each was either fat or scrawny. Carlton stepped back into the trees and searched the faces of the men under their hat brims. He recognized them all and was relieved to not see Brent's father's face among them. The town would have given him a few days off.

When the men finished lowering the gate and had tossed their cigarettes over the rail and had driven their orange town trucks away from the boatlanding, Carlton crossed the dam, feeling the vibration of the weathered wood beneath his feet as he walked the catwalk over the open chutes. Water passed below him and flew out in great loud white arcs. Long before he was born, he lost the uncle for whom he was named to this dam. He'd dropped from the catwalk down into one of the chutes, drunk, clutching an innertube from the tire of a Company truck. He was dead of a broken neck before he ever had the chance to drown in the crash of water. There was a photograph of him in a silver frame at Carlton's aunt's house.

He looked downstream at the two men fishing, one false-casting tremendous loops of line too many times before tangling in mid-air. The other was just jiggling his line in the water, not caring one way or the other about fish. Carlton wondered if they knew each other. He looked back to the chute and thought his uncle must have been very hopeless to make himself do a thing like that.

The last boathouse in the row was blue and belonged to the people with the summer place on the island four miles out from the dam. It had been painted recently. Carlton knew he could bring to mind a vision of Brent holding a bucket of paint and a brush, standing where he now stood, but he blinked it away. Brent's footprints might still be there in the dirt.

The protruding sill of the underwater foundation ran the length of the boathouse, half-immersed in water.

Awkward with his paddle, Carlton inched along the beam to where it stuck out beyond the dark square mouth of the building. Beyond the green shadow of the roofpeak, gasoline mixed with water made floating rainbows. He swung himself around and climbed up inside where a big aluminum boat with an Evinrude 45 was tethered to the rail. Yellow life jackets hung in a row on pegs above a line of five red fuel tanks. Carlton nudged one of the tanks with his boot. It was full. He and Brent had stolen the boats from here regularly years ago. Everyone did. It wasn't something anybody cared about.

A canvas double-end canoe lay tipped up against the wall on the other side of the boathouse. He held the gunwale and pulled the canoe up onto his thighs, and like that sidestepped to the rail, turning to ease the canoe down into the dark water. The bow bumped into the side of the aluminum boat and made a hollow *tonk*. He held the canoe in place with his boot as he reached for his paddle and then got in. With a few strong strokes he was out into the sunlight, feeling the dam's slow pull on the water of the lake.

He paddled hard at first, leaning into the strokes, and by the time he reached the tethered floating bleach bottles that marked shallow rocks, he was breathing hard. The sun was hot on his neck, burning his pale skin. He tipped the paddle up and let water run down its length into his mouth and onto his face. The canoe was so flat, it barely rocked, sending tight ripples out across the surface and distorting the view to the green bottom. Its flatness made the paddling slow, but that was okay. After only a few minutes, the palms of his hands were crossed with red lines from paddling and he could see where the blisters would form. He dipped them both in the cold water to take off the burning. Behind him was the town, and on the flat gray span of the lake ahead of him, the island was a distant floating stand of pines cut loose from the green shoreline.

A boat came out of the distance, seeming never to grow larger and then suddenly inflating as it came by. An old man was at the wheel, wearing a checked wool mackinaw even in the hot weather. His face was drawn tight with age and over the water between them, he looked to Carlton like two deep eye sockets with a dark hole for a mouth. The man raised up his slender arm in greeting as they passed each other. Carlton nodded to him and then realized that it probably wasn't enough of a gesture from so far away and so quickly lifted his own arm in the air. He knew he'd seen the man before, but couldn't tell where. They stared at each other until both their heads were turned around over their shoulders.

Waves from the old man's boat came rolling across the flat water and Carlton swung his bow around to break over them squarely. The nose of the canoe rose and fell, splashing a little, and then he knew what he'd see when he reached the island. It came to him like a revelation as he sat waiting for the water around him to become still again. Somehow, he'd known all along. He switched hands, to his weaker left, and put his paddle to the water again. Before the tree trunks on the island became individually discernible, he saw the bright turquoise of Brent's father's open boat pulled up on the beach.

He swished through a patch of lily pads and let the bow of his canoe scrape up onto the rocky beach. A can of Pepsi was bleeding brown wisps of cola into the water where it floated in the stern of Brent's father's Whaler amongst cigarette ends and a few dead waterbugs. Carlton stepped into the water and set the can upright on the seat plank.

There was a shack just under the trees with a bunch

of long fishing poles hung on nails driven into the cedar shingles. The fittings would tarnish if somebody didn't take them in before winter. He fingered the smooth curve of a metallic minnow, its treble hook securely stuck in the rod's cork handle. Beyond him, under the shade of tall trees, the entire surface of the island was covered in moss and red pine needles and pockets of hemlock cones. He looked back out across the lake toward the dam, invisible in the distance, and then started up the slope.

Brent's father was sitting sideways on the bench of the long picnic table in the center of the camp, looking right at Carlton as he came up the path. His hat and another can of Pepsi were on the table next to him. Carlton nodded and then looked off to either side as he walked, feeling clumsy, like he was walking funny, his legs stiff. His feet made no sound on the dirt path. He felt like a little boy.

When he looked up again, Brent's father was looking off through the trees at the water all around. His belly rested on his lap. His beard had gone gray. Carlton sat down on the other side of the table, trying to make hello come out of his mouth.

Brent's father said, "I thought you might turn up."

They sat like that for quite a while, each looking off through the trees, at the water, at the sky.

In time, Brent's father said, "You know why he did this?"

Carlton shook his head.

"No? Me either." His voice had grown weaker in the years since Carlton had last heard him speak, sounding more like throaty breathing than words. He said, "You believe what you said at church?"

"I did think about it a lot."

"He felt like he'd made a whole life, did he?"

"Is that what I said?"

He nodded.

"He must have."

Brent's father fingered the tab of his can. His cheeks had gone red and he was blinking. "If he did, he was wrong."

A squirrel leapt up onto the far end of the picnic table and sniffed around, its movements jerky, impossibly quick.

"I've been coming out here every day since. It's a nice place."

"We used come out here sometimes. Break in."

"It feels about a hundred miles from anywhere else."

"He told me he'd live here if he could." Carlton wasn't sure Brent had ever said anything like that, but he said it anyway.

Brent's father breathed in and then breathed out. He got a cigarette from his shirt pocket and lit it with a plastic lighter. He turned his head and looked at Carlton.

"You know he hung himself with a log chain?" Carlton nodded. He didn't know the chain part. "If I can figure any of it, I can't figure that. I don't know where he did it either. I've looked around trying to figure where, but you can't tell. I even looked at tree limbs for scuff marks." He drew on his cigarette and the squirrel bounded off the table to the doormat on the main house's step. It was green plastic grass with a plastic daisy and the word WELCOME on top. "Wes Maclean already got hired to do the maintenance. You know that?"

Carlton said, "He'd better take in those fish poles. They're going to rust," and Brent's father didn't say anything for a long time.

They watched the squirrel run from one place to another. Carlton wondered what would make a squirrel leave the shore, risk drowning or brave the ice to get to the island. His stomach made a sound and he wished that he'd eaten something. He still had to paddle the whole way back in this heat. Heat made for a lack of appetite, but he wished he'd eaten at least something.

Brent's father said, "I wish to God he hadn't done this. I don't know anything about anything."

After a while, they got up and walked down to the boats. The shadows had turned around and the silhouette of the treetops darkened the quiet waves that came under the lily pads and up over the rocks on the beach.

Brent's father lifted the bow of his Whaler and pushed the boat out into the water and watched it floating there. "How much longer are you around?" he asked.

Carlton shrugged. "A few days I think."

"Then what?"

Carlton looked at Brent's father, who was staring right back at him, scared to death.

"I don't know yet."

Brent's father stepped into his little boat. Under his weight, it drifted out from the rocks. He pulled the Mercury motor to life and sat down behind the steering wheel, waving with the back of his hand as the Whaler cut an arc through the lily pads. He didn't really look at Carlton, who stood by the shack, not really looking out across the water.

When the sound of the Mercury was almost gone, he looked out after Brent's father and said, "It's okay. I didn't know him either."

THE COMPANY OF

NEIL PEARSON

HOPE is Donny's wife. All she ever wants now is to listen to Waylon Jennings. She's got every one of his records and has bought the available ones all over again on compact discs. Strangers she meets on the computer send her illegal tapes they've made at his concerts. She flies to see him in New York, Toronto, Sante Fe—gone for a week at a time and not home for long in between.

She's wealthy from the timber holdings and Christmas tree plantations her father left her after dying of a record-breaking cardiac arrest. Hope says that you can read about her rich father's death in most thorough medical texts: something like 98 percent blockage in each passage to and from the heart. I haven't seen it, but I believe whatever she says. She has, among other things, a seven-minute home movie of Buddy Holly playing a concert in Evanston, Illinois in 1958. She bought it from a man in Trenton, New Jersey for an unimaginable amount of money. Once, for me, she moved the paintings aside to project moving light onto the bare wall. She pointed out the nervous kid playing the bass guitar. "That's him!" she said, mashing her palms together. I had to agree because she knows her facts, but I was worried the bulb would scorch through the brittle old celluloid.

Donny only does about three things. One is mope. Another is split wood. Hope and Donny have enough split wood to get them through ten winters. In the summer Donny is often outside my own house, which is right across the paved road from his, unloading logs from the back of his one-ton with a mean, little-mouthed look on his face. If I try to talk him out of it, he scowls and then starts splitting the logs into firewood. He knows my stove is small. All the logs are cut to size. Most of the wood he splits will rot back into the earth before it ever sees fire.

I've known Donny since we were six years old. I've known Hope even longer.

Hope will tolerate The Highwaymen impatiently. She saw them at the Knickerbocker Arena and again the next night at the Fleet Center down in Boston during their last reunion, but she finds the whole thing somewhat insincere. It's a poor substitute for a regular Waylon Jennings

performance. Nothing against Johnny Cash or espe-
cially Willie Nelson, but to her, it seems packaged.
"Someone tries to dress them up to look cutthroat."
Plus, she has very little use for Kris Kristofferson. After
Hartford, she abandoned the rest of their tour and lived
in a hotel on Block Island for a week.

Donny doesn't listen to music. He took the radio out
of the one-ton and put it on top of the trash pile six
months ago.

They tried to have a baby once, in years gone by, when
ATCS were the vital marrow of life around here. Everybody in the world owned a red Honda three-wheeler.
But I didn't care for them and was glad when they were
finally made illegal. They seem like a corruption of a
finer form: stout and wide and any idiot could hold a
wheelstand for twenty yards. But Donny disappeared to
Shelton's anyway and came back with two of them. The
doctor thought maybe it was the shock of bumping over
rocks and stumps on her Honda Big Red that caused
Hope to miscarry.

I understand. I did eight years on the AMA Supercross
circuit, 650 class, full Team Green sponsorship. My kid-
neys got so they were like little heart attacks. They hurt

when I took a step, hurt when I rolled over in bed. They hurt when I pissed blood into the toilet. I'd have to get up and put my back under the hot water from the shower for two hours in the middle of the night. I know what shock is all about.

Now I have a Hodaka Combat Wombat 125 which never pretends to be otherwise than a bald-tired weakling. It's under the sheetmetal shed roof that Donny nailed up awning-style behind my house so I'd get all the debris off my front yard and out of his view. I don't even ride fast, just cruise up and down between the rows of baby Christmas trees. Motorcycles will not be the death of me.

Hope doesn't care that Waylon did that Taco Bell ad. She says he's earned the right to make good money. Same for Pizza Hut. At least he writes his own music, which nobody on the radio ever does.

The third thing Donny does is fix engines. He does that as well as anybody. When he was only seventeen, he sunk a Peugeot motor into the frame of a Willys jeep. You're not supposed to be able to do that. Donny's father took a Polaroid and, though I don't know where he got the address, sent it off to the engineers at Peugeot in

France. They were very excited in an even-keeled, European businessman sort of way. They sent Donny, seventeen years old, a plane ticket to Paris. It seems they were interested in the prospects of four wheel drive. I think maybe he should have done it, but Donny says he has no regrets as far as that's concerned. What he did instead was drive around America in a green-painted Econoline, hauling two motorcycles in a Wells Fargo trailer. He could make them fast and unfailing. I could ride them well enough to keep my name in the magazines.

There has been much mythology made of motorcycles and what they mean. Perhaps that explains why I see so many college students and physicians riding new Harley-Davidsons up and down Route 10 where it runs between my house and Donny and Hope's. Anybody with a few dollars in their pocket can buy a motorcycle. I don't see the romance.

Last winter, November twenty-ninth, Hope was in Atlanta with a second-row seat. That was toward the beginning—maybe the fourth or fifth time. She claims that Waylon took off those wraparound glasses and winked at her with recognition in his eye. I suppose it's possible. But I know that if you look hard enough for something that isn't there, you're probably going to see it anyway.

As for me and Donny, we took his Western Star to a Christmas tree distributor on the west end of Long Island. Donny drove. He fixed the hydraulic boom and rebuilt the PTO before he married Hope. That was a long time ago, and it still runs smooth. I can't move too fast or pivot well, but I'm still strong (one hundred push-ups and sit-ups every morning of the year) and I helped him unload hundreds of eight-year-old spruces onto the hot pavement. Not counting the expenses of diesel and food, we made almost nine thousand dollars in green cash. You can sell a Christmas tree, retail, in New York for seventy-five dollars. People will do anything with their money.

Hope does love Donny. They have been together since the tenth grade (not including the time he and I spent on the road—which was, I admit it, a lot). Last October I was walking in the tree-lot behind their house with Hope. It was one of those perfect autumn days we have here, blue blue sky, and she said, "My father died for money."

Her father was not a merciful man. There are stories about that. I said, "Oh?"

"He didn't like it as much as people think. If I'd had a

mother, she would have saved him. He was a lovely, lonely man." She picked up some dirt and let it fall back to the ground. The breeze blew it sideways a little bit.

"Why do you have to go to so many Waylon Jennings concerts all the time?"

She spread her arms wide and I felt all the years I'd known her pass through me. "I get sick of looking at Christmas trees forever." Then she turned and we walked back through the rows toward the sound of Donny's axe breaking hard logs apart.

I'm mostly used up. When I was twenty-five I broke just about everything. If you ask anybody who ever rode the Supercross circuit in my era, they'll tell you about the Stepladder Doubles at the Coronado Raceway in Imperial Beach, California. It was a legendary obstacle, and for a time I became a legend by breaking my body all over the face of the second hump. Kawasaki redesigned their competition forks after mine folded under me and married my body to the dirt. I made the last page of *Moto-Cross Digest*, where, to this day, they publish a photograph of comic personal disaster. The Stepladder Doubles became known, for a while anyway, as Pearson's Stepladder, for Pearson is my name. When the Coronado closed in 1987, the name seemed to contract back to Stepladder Doubles in everybody's remembrance. That doesn't rankle me, especially. Though I can imagine how it might someone else.

One half of my pelvis is made from sculpted plastic. I have lightweight steel in my head. My wrists are another story altogether. These are facts that wouldn't be if the growth rate of technology were a dozen years slower than it is.

I went to Nashville, racing, the same year as my accident. There is nothing *country* about it. Half a million people live in Nashville, spread out from where its settlers must have come ashore from the Cumberland River, their descendents waiting tables, manufacturing ball-bearings, trading stock, drinking wine, going to see indoor motorcross and whatever else. I never saw a horse in Nashville, much less a cow for somebody to punch. Hope agrees. She says Waylon was never truly welcome there. The pageantry didn't mix with his honesty. But I think Texas is mostly bullshit, too.

The town where Donny and Hope and I live has gone by. I don't even know anybody here anymore. New York and Connecticut have bled their people north. My mother is dead and my father has moved to Titusville, Florida where, from his front step, he imagines he can see the space shuttle take off from the Kennedy Space Center. I haven't seen him in almost six years, haven't talked to him since Christmas. I eat just about every meal at Donny and Hope's and try to avoid the store as much as possible. My world is small now. But I have the house that Hope bought for me and it doesn't owe me anything.

That time Donny and I went to Long Island with all those Christmas trees, he gave me two thousand dollars and then put half of what remained in an envelope. The other half went into his jacket pocket. When we got home, he parked the truck behind his house and we got drunk on beer. In the middle of the night, Donny made me drive him to his great aunt Charlotte's house on the Hodaka. It's a small bike and he kept having to get off so I could make it up the hills. He was all smiles for the first time in months, jogging up the road behind me, jubilant in my rearview, bottles of Labatt in his pants pockets, making his hips' silhouette wide against the moon-bright snow.

Below Charlotte's little leaning house, he told me to stop. I did, and leaned the bike against a phone pole. We giggled our way across her cow field and made snow angels with our arms and legs, lay there with snow all around, cutting us off from each other, from everything but the black sky up above. After a while, he got up and put the envelope full of money into the old woman's mailbox. When he came back to me where I lay, counting stars until I reached one hundred, he was crying a little. I didn't ask him what use she'd have for all that money, but he said, "She's so old. She's so good-hearted." Then we walked all the way home through the clean winter air and the Hodaka stayed there in the snowplow pile-up for a month before we went and twitched it out with the Western Star. Even if I make it myself, I can't look at a snow angel without thinking: female.

I ruined myself against the Stepladder Doubles because my hold on the handlebars was too loose. I was entirely relaxed. Hope came out to San Diego to see me in the hospital. A few days later, when I was on the sun deck looking out over the water trying/failing to see Hawaii, she and Donny came by to tell me they were finally getting married. I cried myself, then, because it was so magnificent right there with no other invalids on the deck and the bright promise of California all around. They wheeled me to the Justice of the Peace so I could bear witness to their union like a best man. Donny left the van and the trailer in long-term parking at LAX, sent Kawasaki news of their whereabouts in the same envelope as my hospital bills. We all flew home together. I finished my rehabilitation at the old Mary Hitchcock Hospital before they cut down a few square miles of trees in Lebanon to rebuild it in the architectural style of a shopping mall. Insurance paid for everything.

Donny says that Hope might leave for a Waylon show and stay gone, that she might fall in love with a stranger in a distant city. He says it like he's serious, but I know he doesn't believe it. I miss her too, when she's away. One thing that is clear—all each of us really has is the others. Or I, at least, have nothing else.

Something about the Christmas tree business is that you need commitment. When somebody, in the five years you spend waiting for the little trees you've planted to reach salable size, says "What do *you* do?" you have to be able to answer, with a straight face, "I raise Christmas trees!" You have to believe it yourself.

When one year becomes the next and winter really

takes hold and there is no lasting light, I sometimes don't see Donny and Hope for up to a week at a time. I eat canned soup and sit in my house, moving as little as possible. If you start moving, that's when you realize the limitations of your space and start wanting to claw all the plaster out of the walls. I have a big pile of the wood Donny cut for me stacked up by the stove all year round, and when those dark days of February come, I start feeding them to the flames.

I can see lights in their windows across the road and I start to wonder what they do without me.

What I do is race motorcycles in my brain. It has nothing whatever to do with nostalgia. It's more a trial of memory: the faithful reconstruction of the tracks on the circuit, the loud sounds of hardworking motors, the taste of dust. When I am really there, I'm capable of feeling that blissful vertigo that comes with riding a well-tuned motorcycle high into space.

I can relive my accident, too, if I choose. Most sufferers of head injury lose memory of the incident and the time before as well. I haven't lost a minute. In the ambulance, I scared the emergency technicians by blinking. They had to knock me out to preserve their own composure. When I remember that part, the ambulance, the sound of the siren, something gets switched around. I see myself, on a collapsed gurney, my race gloves still on my hands, my helmet on my head, caved-in on one side. I see what they had to see.

Right now, Hope is down in Austin, Texas for Waylon's final show of the tour. She promised to bring me back a nice t-shirt or a hat. Donny is behind his house. From where I sit, I can hear the cut of the axe, the *clunk* of the split wood as he tosses firewood on the pile. When he's done, he'll pull the whole engine from the one-ton with his block and tackle and stay up all night long, cleaning it until there's not a trace of filth. Or maybe he'll go murder a few more trees. Later still, he'll come across the road and we'll enjoy the last warm moments of the year before it turns cold and snowy.

Many thanks to Jonathan Rabinowitz,
Jeff Clark, Leslie Daniels, Kerrie Mathes,
Aili Dalton, Kathryn Davis, Sarah Ryan,
Pascal Spengemann, Arthur Bradford,
Neil Giordano, Stefan Schaefer, Jim
McPherson, Annie Fitch, Crow Bookshop,
Jordan Lea, Robin Barone, and my little
sisters: Erika, Sydney, and Catherine
for their support and friendship.

Thanks, more than ever,
to Syd Lea and Carola Lea.